The Bridge Out of Town

Jake MacDonald

Acknowledgements: "Vagabonds" was first published in *NeWest Review.* "Two Yellow Pails" originally appeared in *Descant* and *Heartland.* "The Window" first appeared in *Prairie Fire.* "The Bridge" was first published in *Manitoba Stories.* "Reuben" was originally published in *Descant* and "Norris" first came out in *Arts Manitoba.*

ISBN 0 88750 618 6 (hardcover)
ISBN 0 88750 619 4 (softcover)

Cover art by Mina Forsyth. Book design by Michael Macklem

Printed in Canada

PUBLISHED IN CANADA BY OBERON PRESS

For Carolyn

Vagabonds

When I was a kid my family bummed all over the place. My dad was a lawyer who had a touch of the vagabond in him; he was often, as he would say, "between jobs." For a few years we were fairly settled, living in Toronto. Then the same old thing happened and I came down to the kitchen one Saturday morning to find my mother on the phone, crying. The FOR SALE sign went up on the lawn. We loaded the car with everything we owned. I remember staring out the window as we drove out of town. I remember driving up along the north shore of Lake Superior, with my little sister belly-

5

aching and asking when we were going to get there, and I remember wondering what this new home would be like, this place he was dragging us off to. The next day we came to a place in the road where there were police cars and white smoke. The policeman leaned in the window and said that we couldn't continue, there was a forest fire, but my father just smiled and joked with the policeman for a few minutes, then he shifted the car into gear and we drove on, past the emergency vehicles, into a swirling white nothingness. We drove through the white flame-flickering limbo for minutes and minutes and when we came out the other side it was like we'd entered another world. Everything was smoking, black and burned. Later that night we arrived in the little riverside town of Keewuttunnee, which was going to be our new home.

Our new house was just outside of town, a little ramshackle place with a plywood addition attached to the upstairs and a weedy yard going down to the river. There was no basement and the toilet discharged an awful smell when you stepped on the pedal. Looking back on it, I realize now that the house and property were all right by Keewuttunnee standards but for me we'd taken an awful downturn in life. My father went around humming to himself as if this were a grand adventure. I spent the first couple of weeks wandering around the property, hitting the ground with a stick. I couldn't think of a single thing to do with myself. There was no place to swim, unless you counted the river, which was cold and weedy and full of bloodsuckers, and school was out so I had no way of meeting any of the local kids. One night I heard my mother and father arguing. My father said, "I don't want any son of mine growing up with those kind of values." I hated listening to them argue. My father always assumed that the world would be a better place if everyone were more like him.

Every morning my father went to work. He'd joined up with some little two-man local law firm and the phone calls

6

were starting again. The phone would ring at two in the morning and there'd be some drunk person on the phone, asking for Lee Morrison. Even if there were no calls during the night he was usually off to work before I got up. I'd have breakfast and my mother would send me out to play. My mother was on a big short-pants kick that summer. Every day there was a different type of short pants on the bed. Today madras short pants with white woollen socks and canoe shoes. Yesterday white cotton short pants and clean white tennis shoes. Tomorrow probably pink pumps and knee-highs.

I'd finally made a friend, a deaf-and-dumb boy named Dim Harrison who lived two lots down the road, and although he was only about half my size and we could only communicate with hand signals he shared with me a certain sense of revolutionary zeal. We stole our dads' tools and built a tree fort that became our base of operations. We made personal bazookas, which were wicked weapons fashioned from a length of two-by-four and a crosspiece and long strap of inner-tube rubber. We raided neighbourhood gardens for ammo. From where we lay in ambush beside the road, a squeezed trigger on the bazooka would mean a slight twang and a green tomato exploding wonderfully against the windshield of a speeding sports car or dumptruck. We had other weapons as well—spears, slingshots, flimsy bows and arrows that would shoot a twig about twenty yards... even a half-constructed deadfall pit with sharpened stakes and a camouflaged covering of interlaced branches. But our own weapons suddenly seemed pretty pathetic the day we met Bobby Lockland.

The Lockland family were rich tourists who maintained a big summer camp down the road from us. I'd already seen Mr. Lockland a couple of times. He had a little moustache like a movie star and wore a yachting cap and drove a big fancy boat with a silver air horn that honked like a Buick. For a birthday present, he'd given his son Bobby a telescope-sighted semi-automatic .22, every kid's dream. That's the kind of guy he was, not so popular with the parents maybe but a hero with the kids. One day, in the heat of a hazy-quiet July morning, me and Dim were sitting around in the tree fort when we heard voices coming along the road. Quick as cats, we grabbed our bazookas and crept through the woods to our ambush location. It was Bobby Lockland coming. His sister Tricia was trailing along behind him. It wasn't what Bobby was doing, it wasn't what he was saying. It was what he was carrying.

We dropped our weapons and stepped out of the brush. I lifed my hand and attempted a neighbourly grin. "Hi you guys. Is that a real gun?"

"Look at Sam's funny short pants," sneered Tricia, who was a skinny little thing with pointy boobs and a smart mouth. "Is that what communists have to wear?"

"Damn right it's a real gun," said Bobby, ignoring his sister. Bobby's blond hair was neatly cantilevered out over his forehead, like the jutting bumper of one of his dad's cars. He wore wraparound plastic sunglasses and white jeans and walked with an exaggerated saunter, like Cookie Byrnes on 77 Sunset Strip, the guy everyone was trying to look like that summer.

They were walking purposefully along, as if headed out on some no-nonsense mission. I fell in alongside Bobby, and looked at the gun. It was like a piece of expensive furniture, all rich gleaming smooth wood. Not to mention the engraved receiver and the bulbous telescopic sight. I'd never seen anything so beautiful and deadly. "What is it, a semi-auto?"

Bobby nodded. He was two years older and by rights he shouldn't even have been talking to me. But he couldn't resist a respectful fan. "Eighteen hollow points...as fast as you can pull the trigger."

"Wow."

Tricia glanced unenthusiastically at Dim. "Doesn't he

8

ever blow his nose?"

"Did you ever shoot anything with it?"

"Lots of stuff."

"Hey dumb-bell...didn't you ever hear of Kleenex?"

"You ever shoot any squirrels and stuff?"

"You should see all the squirrels he's shot," commented Tricia. "You go out for a walk and you see these dead squirrels lying all over the place. It's really tacky."

"You think you could shoot a bear with it?"

He patted the stock. "Sure...I could stop a bear, if I had to. But you don't shoot them until later in the summer. It's not sporting."

"I know where there's some bears," I said.

"Oh yeah?"

"Yes...my dad and me saw them at the dump. A mother and two babies."

Tricia snorted. "Sam Morrison, you suck. You're a bee-esser."

I broke off a willow switch and glared at Tricia. "Check out," I said. "Or I'll flog ya."

Bobby looked at me. "Was there really some bears?"

"No b.s. There was three of them. Maybe more. Eh Dim?"

I smacked Dim and made the sign for three bears. He nodded quickly. He'd been there, but I don't know if he'd actually seen anything. A quick glimpse was all we'd had in the dark. "I should go give 'em a try," Bobby said, settling the rifle in the crook of his arm. "My old man could use a bear head for the wall of his office."

"Oh gawd...the ultimate in tacky," said Tricia.

I liked the idea. Bear hunting. Yeah...this was the big time. "Let's go over there and have a look," I suggested, trying not to sound excited. "I could show you where they are. Really...you could get 'em easy."

"Yeah?"

Tricia sounded a warning note. "Bob-by...you know

what will happen."

Bobby glanced at his watch. "We can't go over right now. I gotta take my stupid sister water-skiing." Bobby usually talked about Tricia as if she were in another province. "Maybe tomorrow."

"Great," I said. "Me and Dim will wait for you right here. You know our tree house?"

He sort of hesitated for a minute. I probably shouldn't have mentioned the tree house. It probably just didn't sound right, going bear hunting with a couple of kids who still play in a tree house. "Or...maybe we'll meet you on the road here."

"Maybe," he said.

He was already walking away.

"Me and Dim will wait for you right here tomorrow," I shouted after him. "Anytime you want, we'll be here."

Maybe they weren't listening. It sounded like he and Tricia had gone back to arguing.

I was twelve years old and hadn't yet learned how to act the opposite of how you feel. At breakfast the next morning my mother noticed I was keyed up about something. "Where are you off to today?"

I chewed my toast cautiously. "Nowhere."

"You're not planning on going to the dump, I hope."

I stared straight ahead. Had someone been spying on us? Maybe it was something I'd tracked in on my shoes. There was no way of knowing. My mother was a detective the equal of a Sherlock Holmes. "The dump?" I said, buying time with a sip of milk.

"Yes, the dump," she said. "The place where they put garbage. The place you and your friend visit at every opportunity. Were you planning on going there this morning?"

"Uh...I'm not sure."

"Well...I'd rather you didn't go to the dump. All right?"

I nodded.

I laced on my sneakers and went out to call on Dim. We went to the tree fort and waited for Bobby Lockland for an hour or so. To hell with this noise, I finally decided. We continued on to the dump, thinking that probably he'd gone there without us. My mother had only said that she didn't *want* us going to the dump; she hadn't forbidden me to go there. When we arrived, the dump was deserted, nothing but a bunch of ravens and seagulls wallowing around in a sea of trash. The sun beat down. The super-heated air of summer hung motionless, so fouled with the smell of decomposition that you had to screw your face up to breathe it. We walked around, chucking rocks. Dim threw a rock at an old stove and a gopher skittered out, chattering, and dived into his hole. We followed the road that wound through the dump, steep-walled garbage pits falling off on both sides. Half the people didn't even bother throwing their garbage down into the hole. Afraid of bears, they just threw their garbage out of the back of the car and hurried away. Me and Dim poked at the bags with our spears, amazed by the seething maggots and millions of flies. There was a refrigerator down at the bottom of the hole with a constellation of .22 holes in it. I pointed to it. "I wonder if Lockland did that." Dim scrambled down the slope to look at the fridge. He was deaf as a post but I always talked to him anyway.

At the bottom of the pit there was a jungle of rusted-out car bodies, which we checked out, and then a trail leading through a forest of willows and bulldozed trees. We checked out the trail. It led into the woods, the ground got soft and the woods got gloomy. We were slipping through a barbed-wire fence when I noticed a weird-looking footprint in the mud. It was like a bear's footprint, flat and wide, but it had the five toes of a human's bare foot. And it was huge. I pressed my own foot down into the track and covered only half of it. I suddenly felt uneasy. We'd gone a bit too far into these woods. It was spooky in here, silent with the mumble of hornets. "Dim!" I said, tugging his sleeve. "Look...."

I was pointing to the track and Dim was still trying to twist through the barbed-wire fence and then I heard the sound of something coming. You could hear a grunting sound and the thud of heavy feet. I stood there and stared in the direction of the approaching noise. Dim picked up my alarm and followed my gaze into the bush and at that moment the willows parted and there came galloping out the most frightening thing I'd ever seen in my life. I shouted with terror and grabbed at Dim. His shirt ripped open as he fell free of the barbed-wire and both of us went backwards onto the ground. We both jumped up and ran so fast that our legs almost intertwined. I could hear the crashing of the willows and the terrifying bellow and grunt of the creature behind us. To the end of my days I'll never forget that face, purple and scarlet and horribly disfigured, one eyeball skewed to the left, the nose smashed sideways, the mouth open and snaggle-toothed and swinging with drool; I'd seen a few scary movies but it was the first time in my life I'd encountered a real living breathing monster.

Fifty feet away the 7-Up bottle exploded.

Bobby Lockland stood beside me, peering at his handiwork through the telescopic sight. He lowered the rifle and looked at me and Dim. "You guys are full of b.s.," he said.

"Honest to God," I protested. "We saw it with our own eyes."

"You saw a seven-foot tall monster with sharp teeth and a purple face," he mimicked.

We both nodded. Dim made a fluttering series of hand signals. "He says maybe it's a sasquatch," I interpreted, after guessing what Dim was getting across. "We saw a show about them on television."

We were on the lawn out behind Lockland's palatial summer home. There was a tether-ball and volleyball court at one end of the huge backyard and a recently installed rifle range for Bobby down at this end. Bobby had killed all the squirrels within walking distance of the house and now he was reduced to blowing up liquor and soda-pop bottles, which the laughing adults down on the verandah kept him supplied with in good quantity.

"Okay," he finally said. "We'll go to the dump tomorrow morning and check it out. But you guys better not be jerkin' me around," he said, snapping the action on the gun. "Or you're going to be sorry."

The next morning was Saturday, and I almost got sucked into helping my dad haul stones for the new dock, but I managed to slip away before he got around to asking me. I called on Dim and we walked along the winding country road to the hydro right-of-way where we'd agreed to meet Bobby. I couldn't believe it when we came around the corner and he was actually there, standing there waiting for us with the .22 tucked under his arm. We ran up to meet him. "You guys better not be lying," he said.

"Honest. You'll see. Is your gun loaded?"

"Never mind about that," he said. He looked at us up and down, like a general surveying his troops. He pointed to Dim's trailing shoelaces. He shook his head. He was wearing wire-rimmed sunglasses and he looked like one of those cool air-force cadet guys. "Okay," he said. "Let's move."

We walked the mile and a half to the dump. On the way, Bobby took a few shots at a hornet's nest we spotted in the branches of a tree, also a few harmless shots at a striped gopher that paused momentarily in its sprint across the road. He explained that you always shoot at the road in front of a gopher, then you get him on the ricochet. It's more of a challenge, he explained. In any case the gopher got away unscathed and we continued on. When we got to the driveway into the dump Bobby motioned for us to keep quiet and stay behind him. He clicked the safety off his rifle and moved ahead, tiptoeing. The dump was stifling hot,

13

deserted, not even a crow or a vulture in sight. The only sound was the lazy mumbling of flies and the rabbit-thump of my heart. We stalked down the road, past the garbage pits, and stood for five long silent minutes on a knoll above the car bodies. Finally there was a rattle of a tin can down the slope and a gopher scurried out. "Is that your monster?" Bobby said.

He was trying to sound sarcastic but you could tell he was a bit relieved. He drew a bead on the gopher but it ducked out of sight just as he pulled the trigger. BANG. A bottle exploded and the gopher scampered down the hill. "Oops, you missed," I said.

"Damn it!" he exclaimed. "Don't move when I'm shooting!"

He jogged down the hill after the gopher. It scurried under a pile of lumber. Dim and I followed Bobby as he approached the pile of lumber. We heard the gopher chatter derisively inside. It poked its head out between two boards and Bobby fired, missing again even though the gopher was only five or six feet away.

"There's its hole," I shouted, pointing to a burrow in a sand bank not far away. "Don't let him get to his hole!"

The gopher, as if understanding English, spurted out of the lumber pile and galloped toward the burrow. Bobby threw his rifle up and commenced firing. The gun spat bullets in a deadly staccato drum roll and the dirt flew up and spurted and exploded all around the gopher as he ran a broken-field pattern to the burrow. The last bullet hit the sandbank and the chamber clicked empty as the gopher winked into the hole. I looked at Bobby, shaking my head. Eighteen bullets in a couple of seconds. I could have kayoed that gopher with a slingshot.

There was obviously no point in being stealthy anymore. We poked around the brush piles and kicked the doors of the rusted-out automobiles, hoping to flush another varmint. Dim waved excitedly, pointing at the dirt. I went over and saw that he'd discovered another footprint. I called to Bobby. "Look...."

He came over and looked. His fingers drummed the wooden forepiece of the gun. "So that's your man-creature," he said. "Probably just some bush-neechie with no shoes to wear."

I circled around. "There's more tracks going down the sandbank over here," I announced. "A whole bunch of them. Maybe the creature uses this as a trail."

Bobby followed the footprints down the slope, past the car bodies, up to the barbed-wire fence where Dim had ripped his shirt. He slipped through the fence and tiptoed forward, looking into the willows on his left and his right. Me and Dim hung back. He looked back over his shoulder, hissing. "Are you guys coming or not?"

Once you got away from the trash and the smell of the dump, the trail through the woods was quite pleasant. The path went downhill to a bubbling creek, and then meandered along the edge of the creek where it was all mossy and silent. We tiptoed along, following Bobby. The ground was mottled with patches of sunlight and the air was sweet with the smell of flowering cottonwood trees. Bobby stiffened his arm suddenly in a cautionary signal. He sank to one knee and we did the same. He reached forward and pulled a screening branch gently out of the way. Just ahead, on a sunlit bench above the miniature river, there was a little shack made out of scrap lumber and roofing plastic, with a front door made out of an old sheet-metal Coca-Cola sign. On a tripod in front of the shack a big fire-blackened kettle hung above the dead embers of a camp fire. Bobby glanced meaningfully at us, raising his finger to his lips. We studied the scene for several minutes, searching for some sign of life. A whisky-jack flew down and landed on the tripod above the fire pit. The black roofing plastic bagged and puffed lazily in the summer breeze. Bobby stood up. "Let's check it out."

We went to the shack and poked around. Bobby looked

inside. "There's two people living here," he said.

We joined Bobby at the doorway and looked inside. There were two cots inside, made of two-by-four frames and chicken wire. Along one wall was a complex of shelves made from stacked wooden crates. On the shelves were old paperback novels, tin plates and cups, candles, a row of old photographs, a car battery wired up to a push-button automotive radio. On a hood above each cot was a dangling CNR lantern. Bobby moved inside and snapped on the radio. Music surged out. *I've crossed the deserts bare, man, I've breathed the mountain air.* Bobby grinned at us, snapping his fingers. He thumbed through a couple of books and threw them on the cot. Dim and I joined him. "Who do you suppose lives here?" I asked.

"Hoboes," Bobby said.

I'd heard of hoboes but had never seen one before, let alone been inside a hobo house. Dim picked up one of the little framed photographs from the shelf. It was a very old portrait of a woman in a high collar dress, with a baby on her knee. The baby wore a fancy lace bonnet. Another picture showed a young man in a soldier's uniform. Bobby took the picture away from Dim and studied it. "That's not a Canuck uniform," he said. "These guys must be foreigners. Russians or something."

I was a bit uneasy. Russians? And we're in here poking around in their bedroom? If they came home unexpectedly God knows what they'd do to us. Bobby went back outside and we quickly followed him. "Look at this," he said, kicking at a tin can. "Dog-food can. These guys eat dog food. Is that tacky or what?"

He picked up the can and read the label, shaking his head. He handed me the can. "Throw it up in the air."

I threw the can and he fired as it tumbled down amongst the trees. The gun made a startlingly loud slap in the little clearing.

"Stand back," Bobby said.

Holding the gun casually at his hip, he pointed at the kettle suspended from the tripod. Dim and I backed off. The gun spat three times and a row of holes erupted on the kettle's sides. Triple streams of dark liquid peed out, sizzling in the dead ashes. "Now check this out," he said.

He machine-gunned a dozen round into the door and walls of the shack. We could hear plates and glass exploding inside. We laughed. You had to be there. It was quite irresistibly funny. "Can I have a try?" I said.

Bobby loaded the gun with trembling fingers. He handed it to me. I took the rifle and stepped forward. I pressed the trigger and the gun, totally obedient, spat a bullet into the hut. I fired twice, then as fast as I could pull the trigger. The noise and the burnt-match smell of gunpowder filled the clearing. Then it was Dim's turn. Bobby giggled maniacally, loading the gun. We both laughed as Dim ran up to the hut and kicked the door open and sprayed inside, just like Sergeant Rock. Bobby took the gun away from Dim. "Okay...let's get out of here," he said.

We began walking quickly up the path.

"Let's cut through the woods to the road," he said. "Just in case somebody heard us."

We began walking quickly through the woods. Then we started trotting. Was that the sound of someone shouting at us? In no time we were running as fast as we could for the road.

Back home my dad was getting ready to haul stones for the new dock. A truck had come and unloaded a huge pile of rock in the backyard. A couple of hired hands were going to come over and help put the stones in the dock crib. I had just finished my lunch and my mother was doing the dishes when there was a loud knock at the front door. I went to the door and nearly filled my drawers. There, looking at me through the screen, was the purple-faced snaggle-toothed monster. I probably made some pathetic whimpering noise as I stepped backwards, expecting a claw to come smashing through the screen, but whatever I did it didn't affect the cheerful expression of the little man who was standing beside the creature. "Afternoon sonny...is your old man around?"

My dad came downstairs and stepped out the door. He greeted the two men, and shook hands with the short one, who said his name was Earl. "This here is Tommy," said Earl. He leaned toward my father slightly. "Don't worry about Tommy," he said in a confiding way. "He's a little slow, but he's all right."

My father stuck out his hand. "Nice to meet you Tommy."

The giant made a grizzly bear gurgle and his eyes swivelled around and he stuck out his paw. My dad shook it. A thread of saliva dangled from the giant's mouth.

"Don't worry," whispered Earl. "Tommy, he'll just help out for a while. Then when he gets tired he'll run on home."

My father nodded. "Fine. Should we have a look at the job then?"

My father walked around the corner of the house, with the old man alongside him and Tommy loping along behind. I followed. My dad led them down the lawn to the riverbank. I should tell you, up here in northern Ontario the rivers don't look like a river down south. A river is like a long chain of lakes, sometimes a mile across. You wouldn't even know it was a river if you didn't have the voyageurs and the Indians and the history books to tell you about it. Anyway, our lawn goes down to the rocky shore, then blue water and green hills as far as you can see. My dad has spiked together these big boxes out of railway ties. You gotta take the rocks and dump them into the boxes, and then you've got a foundation to build your dock on. My dad and Earl started throwing these rocks into the crib boxes, and Tommy just stands there watching them. Earl sort of motions to Tommy, come on, you can help. Tommy picks up a huge

18

boulder and carries it gently, like it's a big goose egg, and lays it down in the crib. Then he goes over and whispers something to Earl.

"Okay," Earl says.

Tommy runs up the lawn, grunting to himself like he has to go to the bathroom or something. Earl carries another rock and throws it into the crib. My dad looks a little concerned. "Is he all right?"

"Oh sure," says Earl. "He's just a little tired already...I told him he could go home."

Later on, my dad took Earl up to the kitchen for a coffee break. Earl took his boots off at the front door and tiptoed into the kitchen like it was a church. He kept nodding to my mother and calling her "missus." Earl was one of these skinny guys with a leathery face, grease rubbed right into the wrinkles of his face like the dirt on a saddle. He'd brought along his own tea bag, which he pulled out of his pocket and gave to my mother, and after he'd sat down he rolled a skinny cigarette and ignited it with an old army lighter that threw a flame about five inches high and reeked of gasoline. My father came in with a bunch of old history books and showed them to Earl. It turns out that my father and Earl were in the same army unit, something called the MacKenzie Papineau brigade, and they were right away off in their own little world, talking about Spain and Franco and all this stuff that happened in the old days. I remembered the picture of the soldier back at the shack, and figured that it had to be Earl. I didn't want to imagine what the inside of that shack looked like after we'd left.

At supper-time my little sister wanted to know who those two funny guys were. My dad said that they were brothers and that their names were Earl and Tommy. He said that they were migrant workers from Saskatchewan. My little sister wanted to know if it was true that they lived at the garbage dump. My dad said that they didn't have much money, so they'd made a little camp for themselves out in

19

the woods. She said, but why do they live beside a garbage dump? My father hesitated for a few moments, sipping his tea thoughtfully the way he does when he's trying to be patient, and explained that we live in a society where people throw a lot of good things away, and a guy like Earl knows how to fix things and make them functional again.

"Which one is Tommy?" asked my sister.

I interrupted. "The one who looks like Frankenstein."

My little sister giggled. My father glared at me. "Tommy had a pot of boiling water spilled on him when he was a baby. Earl takes care of him because he loves him, despite the way he looks. What gives you the right to make fun of them?"

A few days later my father came up to me and asked if I knew where Earl and Tommy's shack was. He had poker-faced lawyer's expression on his face that said, you better tell the truth, because maybe I know the answer already. I nodded in the affirmative, feeling my stomach tie a slow knot. "Come on, we're going for a little car ride," he said.

We drove over to the dump and my father opened the trunk of the car. There were two boxes; he took the heaviest one. We walked through the woods. I led the way, feeling like a condemned prisoner. I had no idea what Earl had said to my father or what he suspected or what was waiting for me up ahead. Pretty soon we saw the smoke of their campfire through the trees and the outline of the shack and the two men sitting by the fire. Neither of them looked the least bit surprised as we walked up with our boxes. You'd think that visitors dropped in like this regularly. Earl nodded mildly. "Well look who's here. Tommy...you remember Lee Morrison? And this here is his son Sam, if I remember correctly...."

I nodded. "Yes sir."

A quick glance around the camp showed no sign of our recent raid. If anything the place looked better. The shack had a verandah nailed onto it and the windows had little flowerboxes made of nail kegs, planted with wild daisies. They'd scrounged a bunch of old bricks and made a nice waist-high brick barbecue, and the kettle sat on top of it bubbling in the blue smoke. The kettle had a row of holes that were plugged with wooden pegs, the only evidence of the hell we'd raised several days ago. Tommy lurched around, gurgling and drooling, while Earl casually sorted through the gifts my father had brought. I sat down on the log bench beside my father. Tommy came out of the shack and tapped me on the shoulder. He handed me a coffee cup. I looked up at his crooked eyes. "Thank you," I said. I looked at the cup. It hadn't been washed recently and the handle was broken off. Tommy handed one to my father. My father was looking around, admiring the campsite. "Thanks Tommy. Say...you fellahs have a nice campsite here. Nice creek nearby. Lots of blueberries, I imagine. Have you had any problems with bears, with the dump so close by?"

"Tommy is on a first-name basis with most of them," Earl said. "He walks right past them, they don't even look up. If a car comes into the dump, Tommy and the bears are falling all over each other scrambling for the woods. You should see it."

Earl unhooked the coffee pot. "Who wants a cup of mud?"

My dad took the tail of his jacket and deftly wiped the interior of his cup. "Hit me."

Earl looked at me. "You want some coffee sonny?"

I wasn't supposed to be drinking coffee but I took a chance. I stuck out the cup. "Sure...hit me."

The swimming-dock was finished and we made it our new headquarters. I'd made some new friends, too. Burt Harrison and an Indian kid named Sonny Copenace and a few other kids were starting to come around. Things were turning out all right after all. At that point I don't think you could have got me back to the city for love or money.

21

One day, Dim and I were catching minnows and we saw Mr. Lockland coming. We'd made a seine net out of lead sinkers and cheesecloth and we were in the water, up to our waists, when we spotted Lockland's big powerful flashy boat coming. Mr. Lockland slowed the boat down and gave us a couple of toots on the air horn, waving for us to get out of his road. He pulled the boat up to the dock and tied up. "Hey sport," he said. "Where's your dad?"

He went up the hill to the house and we followed.

We loitered underneath the kitchen window and listened. "The long and short of it is, Lee...these bums are on public property and they're becoming a nuisance. I've been going around talking to some of the other campers and they seem to share my concern. Now, all I'm asking for is your signature, nothing more."

I could hear my father's dry tone of voice. He could always make it sound like he was the only sensible one. "A nuisance? I don't see them as a nuisance, particularly."

"Well, what about the health hazard?"

My father chuckled.

"You laugh, but really Lee...what are they using for sanitation facilities? Where are they getting their drinking water? I for one don't want to see an outbreak of disease in this community, caused by vagabonds who don't even pay taxes."

"Why don't we go and pay them a little visit...I'll show you how they built this catcher for rain water. It's ingenious as hell. You'll probably go straight home and make one yourself."

"Lee...I don't really want to get into a debate about the quality of their drinking water. We have a couple of legitimate concerns here, and we're asking for your support. Now, this big one, the funny one who staggers and dribbles from the mouth... Is he not quite right? Is he drunk or something?"

"He's not drunk, Carl."

"Whatever he is, I'm concerned about the children, walking these wooded roads unattended. I have a fourteen-year-old daughter to consider. And you have children too."

There was a long moment of silence. Finally my father replied. "Tommy was severely injured in a childhood accident. He's as harmless as a rabbit. He's under the constant supervision of his brother."

"Why isn't he in some kind of institution...where he can be cared for properly?"

"He is being cared for properly."

Mr. Lockland guffawed. "Come on Lee, they live in a garbage dump!"

"Well...they're a bit down on their luck. There's no law against that."

"So you won't sign the petition?"

Dead silence. I could imagine my father shaking his head. The front door banged. We heard Mr. Lockland coming. We ducked into the crawl space under the house and watched his perfectly tailored white slacks swish by.

A few weeks later somebody tipped off the local authorities that Tommy and Earl were illegally squatting on crown land and the Ministry of Natural Resources went over there and told them they'd have to leave. Then the police found out and they went over there too, because they had a warrant for Tommy under the Mental Health Act. It seems that Tommy was absent-without-leave from a mental institution, on the lam with his brother Earl, who was more or less hiding Tommy up here in the north woods hoping nobody would find them. All this I found out from my father as we drove over to the dump that afternoon to offer his services as legal counsel.

When we got to the dump there were two or three government cars there and there was a lot of black dirty smoke coming up from the ravine where they were burning down the camp. There was an OPP cruiser sitting at the edge of the garbage pit and one of the younger cops, John

23

Murphy, was standing there talking to Earl and Tommy. Earl kept shaking his head, no, no, stubborn-looking with his hands on his hips.

"Stay in the car," my father said.

He got out of the car and walked toward them.

I looked past the rising pall of black smoke to the beautiful forested ridge that rose up beyond. Late August, the poplar leaves changing, a pale-blue autumn sky. Another car pulled in behind us and I looked sideways—Bobby and Trish Lockland sitting beside their dad in the front seat of their white T-bird. They swung past and parked, sitting there, not opening the car doors, but just sitting there eye-balling the cop cars and the green-jacketed game-wardens coming up out of the ravine where the camp was burning.

My father walked up to John Murphy and said something and the cop grinned like my dad had cracked a joke. The cop had his arm on Tommy's shoulder like they were old buddies. Anytime anybody said anything Earl just shook his head stubbornly, no. The policeman took his hand off Tommy's shoulder and pulled out a folded paper and handed it to my dad.

Not wanting to miss a single detail of this I just sat in the car, watching.

Two Yellow Pails

One night, in the dead of winter, Chief Romeo Star's son broke into the Keewuttunnee Indian Reserve bank office with an axe and spent most of the night sniffing glue and trying to chop the building to the ground. The next morning the building looked approximately the same as it does now...caved-in wallboards, hacked-up desks and surprisingly neat slots in the hollow core doors where the axe punched clean through. In afterthought, little Bobby Star also added a new colour scheme to the interior of the offices, spray-painting the windows a runny shade of lavatory green, and slopped great hemorrhage-like splashes of red paint in the sag of the swivel chairs where the person's rear end sits. Because of the painted windows, the building from that morning on entered into a state of perpetual, greenish dusk. Nobody ever took on the job of replacing the windows or otherwise correcting the damage, but in some of the offices small palm-sized spyholes were scraped in the dismal finish, admitting entrance to the sunlight and exit to the eye. It was through one of these windows on a window that the local social worker, a young white male named Leonard Nacaratu, was watching a girl at the water pump outside, filling a yellow plastic pail.

Leonard Nacaratu, as he watched her through the window, told himself that he should be getting back to work, not sitting here staring like a lovestruck fool. He hadn't been giving one hundred per cent to his job lately and it seemed to him that this very female was causing all the trouble. He didn't know this girl but felt like he was in love with her, if such a thing were possible. Sometimes this private fascination struck him as being a bit unhealthy, as disquieting as an invalid's glimpse of himself in a mirror. He, Leonard, the sensible, had hauled his massive desk into an oblique position in the middle of the room. From his swivel-chair his eye and the spyhole in the window were now trained, inevitable as a gunsight, on the infirm shape of the girl's house, a mere quarter of a mile away. Watching her now, her gait that he'd memorized, her stride, her modest and straightforward pace that aspired only to cross ground, and watching her toss her head, her pail filling at the tap, her waist-length hair moving as she moved, Leonard was as motionless at his desk as one of the clods of mud at her feet. He knew that it must now be approximately 10.30, morning coffee break, because this was the point on her schedule at which she would usually walk up from her house and fill a plastic pail with water from the well. She would stand there for several minutes, talking in Ojibway to the other women,

26

and then lift the pail and walk back to her house. Leonard, his fair hair, fair skin sheltered from the direct June sun, would polish his glasses and watch quietly from the cigarette-fouled confines of his office, his fingers drumming nervously on the desk.

It had been happening like this ever since winter, with one last assault, had fallen back and retreated from the north country for good. Now morning's light brought the smell of open ground, the racket of crows floating in through his window. Instead of the dull pounding of winter's cold, the granite-coloured sky, the landscape was brightened by base-ball games, new cars, the groups of old women with their bags of groceries and polka-dotted scarves. Leonard had been living on the reserve for almost two years and was beginning to feel quite at home with these cycles. The children, for instance, were no longer just a nameless horde that bubbled and swarmed in the schoolyard every morning like so many minnows. He knew them all by name now, and knew a little bit about each one. There was little Joe Stump, whose father was king trapper of this area and kept many of the old people supplied with moose meat every winter. There was Sarah Land, whose parents both drowned last fall while out rice picking. There was pretty young Jesse Blackbird, who could run faster than any of the boys. And there was little Robert New York, five or six years old, whose father had once been chief and who himself, judging from his fearless smile and love for pow-wow dancing, would probably someday also be chief of this band.

Having developed this familiarity with the people on the reserve Leonard was not entirely looking forward to his departure at the end of June. He'd been hired on a contract basis and it seemed that because of government cutbacks his contract was not to be renewed. This in itself was not a cause for grief. So many others he knew had encountered a similar fate, or indeed had not even encountered the opportunity to work in the first place, that Leonard did not feel too hard

27

done by. How could he, he asked himself, when most of the men from the village would consider themselves lucky to get a job shovelling sand for $4 an hour? Nevertheless, as his departure date neared, Leonard grew more and more down-hearted at the prospect. Simultaneous to these cross-currents of change—the onset of spring, the termination of his contract with its accompanying prospect of having his roots once again torn out before his eyes—Leonard chanced to first lay eyes on the girl with the yellow pail.

He'd always imagined that he knew all of the young women on the reserve, if not by name at least by appearance. It was therefore a jolt for him to one day round a corner in the office and see her standing there, reading from the bulletin board. He could still recall the moment in precise detail, and how when she looked at him, over her shoulder, there followed the most amazing moment of pure recognition, as if they were meeting now as strangers, having known each other very well in some other office hallway, in some other place and time. He went home that night with the remembrance of that incident on his mind. One of his neighbours in the government townhouse said that, yes, he knew the girl in question, and that her name was Rosemary, and that yes, she certainly was attractive, and that, uh, she had an interesting background.... Did he know that?

Leonard walked down to the police trailer that night and Constable Murphy told him about the time that Rosemary Land had killed her husband. It had happened about two years ago, before Leonard arrived, and she had lived in virtual seclusion ever since. The constable thought that she had two kids, both by the dead man. He used to come home drinking, at first just occasionally and then every night. He'd come home and beat her up and wreck the house and rough up one of the kids and then pass out, exhausted. One night he broke Rose's collar-bone and started practising his golf swing with the two-year-old's head against the wall. Rose put him away with a twelve gauge. That's all.

"It was a good killing," the constable concluded. "The sonofabitch deserved it."

Despite the fact that the trial was almost a mere formality, that the press, the police and the judge had been so supportive as to almost break down in tears during parts of her testimony, Rose came back to the reserve bearing the stigma of a murderer. Her husband, for one thing, had been a member of one of the strongest families in the area, while she was a virtual unknown who had originally come from a remote settlement further north. For this reason she had no family to support her, no relatives, and her own penitent attitude made her almost a complete hermit at the age of 25.

After talking to the constable Leonard was even more obsessed by her than before. He would sit impatiently at his desk in the morning, his eye fixed on the hole in the window. After she made her morning appearance at the water pump he would face the rest of the day feeling deflated, as if everything else were going to be just a colossal waste of time. At lunch-time he'd sit out on the sundeck of his lavish cedar dwelling and eat his lunch, staring out at the acres of run-down Indian shacks. One night late, unable to sleep, he padded into the bathroom and shaved. In the last two years he'd grown a full U-shaped beard. Now underneath it he discovered the strained pale face of the ageing government bureaucrat that he'd always dreaded becoming. Watery blue eyes stared back at him, thinning sandy hair, combed back, pale hands freckled across the knuckles...his time was growing short.

So, the end of June came and he packed his possessions into cardboard boxes, neatly taped. One night there was a pow-wow and Leonard was presented with a carved wooden moose as a token of appreciation for his work in the community. He waited all night but the girl named Rosemary didn't show up.

The next day Leonard cleaned up his office. People were already making plans to move into it, introducing their own

29

charts and schedules to the wall. Leonard kept the back door open all morning, admitting the flies and the sunlight and the breeze off the river. It seemed like summer now, and he stood looking out the back door at the car bodies behind the band office, the hip-high weeds growing up through their frames and the hillside and the river down below. A half mile away Rosemary's house, its bile-green finish simmering in the heat, stood as if deserted. Leonard replayed over and over again the few times he'd spoken with her. Once, on a wet day about a week ago, at the mud-caked boot-scraper on the front stairs.

He: "Boy, it sure is a wet day."

She: "Yes."

His other memorable conversation transpired on the road at night about one week earlier. Leonard, on his way to the store to buy Coke and chips for the late movie, was bumping down the pot-holed road in his Volvo under the light of the full moon. Suddenly he saw her in the headlights.

He: "May I give you a ride?"

She (standing against the purple canvas of the night, as lovely as a madonna) "No thank you."

Leonard went over these scenes over and over again, searching her negative responses for the slightest inconsistency. Sometimes he wondered if he were making a monstrous error, and then he would go home and find where the children had scrawled a heart, along with "Rose and Mr. Nukka" on the dusty hood of his Volvo, or he would look up and see her staring at his window as she filled her pail at the well, and he would be right back head-over-heels in love with her again.

So his last day came, and his last day was passing.

He stood in his office, chain-smoking Craven As, looking out the window. His car was loaded and packed and ready to go. He had no sooner resigned himself to getting an early start on the road when a movement caught his eyes and he looked out the window and saw Rose standing there.

She was standing at the well and filling two yellow pails. Leonard came out the door of the office and floated down the steps. Light as a wire, he felt every rib in the concrete-dry earth as he came up behind her.

"Rose," he said.

She flinched, spilling a stripe of water on her jeans.

Leonard looked at her, fighting a sudden vertigo. Here was no dream image. Here was another human being, alive, moving, his own height almost. Her hair, long and thick, contained glints of purple light. Her eyes, faintly yellowed, looked at him from a face with high flat cheekbones, a face of oriental beauty.

"Can I help you with those?" he asked.

She tossed her head in her shy way, indicating no. "It's easier to carry two than one," she said.

That was a good answer, he thought to himself. When you get right down to it it's probably easier to do everything without help.

She tipped her head and began to move away. What was he supposed to say now? He watched her go, feeling as if he'd been struck dumb. He'd never been any good at this sort of thing. When she was 60 feet away a voice tore out of him.

"Rose!"

She stopped. He ran up to where she was standing.

"I was wondering...I have to go back to where I came from, and I just wanted to tell you."

She looked from side to side tightly, as if embarrassed to be caught out in the open like this. She didn't make a habit of flirting with strangers...didn't he know?

"I was wondering if you'd like to go to a movie in Kenora tonight...?"

Her hair tossed in shock. "I can't."

"Then maybe we could go fishing."

"I can't."

"Maybe we could just go for a walk then?"

31

She grimaced. She couldn't imagine such a thing. Everybody would be watching. "I can't go for a walk," she said.

"Maybe I could just visit," he said. His hands were stuck in his pockets. He looked like he could keep this up all night.

"We could go to a movie," she finally replied. "I'll go at 6.30," she said, turning away. She walked quickly back to her house, as if half the reason she'd assented was to escape. Leonard could barely restrain himself from delivering a loud whoop. He jogged back to his townhouse and spent the next hour washing and drying his good pair of blue jeans. Frances, his neighbour, had left a note asking him to drop over and say goodbye. Leonard dodged the note and kept reasonably quiet in his apartment, not wanting to attract the attention of any of his neighbours. They were supposed to have a lot in common, but lately a gap had been developing between him and the rest of the whites on the government payroll here. His solemn interest in Rose seemed a topic of amusement among some of his friends and Leonard had stopped mentioning it, finding himself increasingly uninterested in their world-views and cynical brands of humour. He'd succeeded in having fewer and fewer friends, until now he was alone...just like Rosemary.

By six o'clock it was dusky outside; a summer storm was brewing. Leonard stepped outside, locked his door and put the key in the mailbox. A sullen mob of thunderheads stood piled up in the southwestern sky. Sometimes a thump, faint as the start-up of a distant freight train, could be heard from that same sullen direction. Leonard went down the stairs to his car, observing the charged air, the heavy silence. He got in his Volvo and drove slowly toward Rose's house. It was early but he couldn't wait any longer. He was vibrating like an electrical appliance.

Leonard parked his car in front of Rosemary's cockeyed, leprous-green house and killed the motor. He got out of his car and picked his way across the planks that led to her front door. A sharp-eared German shepherd with a chest like a birdcage threw a torn growl at him and faded under the stairs like smoke. Thunder rumbled distantly as he mounted the steps. The door was mutilated by a thousand clawings from the dog. He tapped the door and stood there, his heart roaring in his ears. The door opened slowly and he was looking down at a fat little three-year-old with button-black eyes.

"Hi there!" he smiled, conscious of being on trial. This would be one of the kids, he thought to himself. "Is your mum home?"

"Eh!?" It was more an exclamation than a query.

"Are you Rose's little boy?"

"Eh!!!?"

"Little girl, then?"

"Huh???!"

The door opened wider and a little girl appeared, slightly older than the boy. "Rosemary's not home."

Leonard stood there. He hadn't thought that this would happen. The possibility had never even entered his mind. For a moment he couldn't speak. "Where did she go?"

The little girl looked back over her shoulder uncertainly. Then she said, "She's gone to east end."

"Thanks," Leonard said. He went back down the stairs and back to his car and accelerated off toward the east end. He had come to pick her up a little early, he thought to himself. Maybe she'd just now be walking home. He drove quickly through the pot-holes and stopped whenever he saw someone, asking if they'd seen her. People were unaccustomed to seeing him drive through this part of the reserve and he received some dubious looks. A drunkard reeled out onto the road and waved his arm at the approaching Leonard, who waved neatly and drove right by. Fifteen minutes later found him back at Rose's house. She was in the backyard, hanging laundry on the line. "Hi," he said.

She regarded him without reply, a shirt knotting and

unknotting in her fists. Leonard stepped toward her, careful of his Hush Puppies in the dog shit. She began to move away. He stopped.

"Would you still like to go to a movie?"

"I can't."

His heart sank. "Why not?"

"I don't have a sitter."

He was relieved. He'd already thought of this. "That's okay. We can take the kids, can't we? There's a good movie playing at the college in Kenora tonight. It's called *RoseMarie*. Have you ever seen it?"

"I can't."

"It's that one, you know, where Nelson Eddy plays this singing Mountie and Jeanette McDonald..."

"I can't go," she quietly interrupted.

"Oh." He thought for a moment. "Maybe we could go for a walk, or just go into Kenora, you know, for something to do, maybe have a milkshake or something...."

"I can't. I have to do the laundry."

"Oh...well, would you like to do something after you've done your laundry?"

"I'll be too tired then."

He nodded. He was getting the drift. She regarded him with large dark eyes, something pained and rigid in their depths. He could barely stand to look at her, her pull on him at this moment was so strong. "Rose..." he began a speech. "I don't know what to do...should I go away, or should I just..."

"My baby is crying," she interrupted. She turned and went into the house.

Leonard stood in the backyard, his hands grinding coins silently in his pockets. The air was heavy and smelled of thunder and a number of mosquitoes were taking turns trying to drill into his scalp. He batted at them and strode up to the backdoor, a growl like a torn truck muffler warning him not to step inside the threshold. The impending thunderstorm made it surprisingly dark inside the house and he stood in the back doorway, looking in at the kitchen where Rose was changing the baby's diapers. One of the kitchen windows was broken and the wind that gusted and puffed through the shattered glass, stirring and sailing papers to the floor of the stark and featureless room, created in Leonard a moment of awful clarity, in which he thought he could see it all—past and future, his fate as well as hers. She was probably right, he thought to himself. The vague plans he'd entertained of them escaping together were probably ridiculous. Could he picture Rose moving with him to the city? Amongst Indian-hating landlords, Me-generation males, women fond of discussing orgasm and the layered look? And could he picture himself, child of affluence, settling in here for an eternity of dirty diapers, brutal poverty and the memory of shotguns going off in the middle of the night?

Leonard stood there for a few more minutes, not speaking, and felt that he was slowly becoming invisible. When his image finally faded, when there was nothing left of where he stood but evening air, he turned and went across the yard and got in his Volvo and drove off down the road. It rained hard all night and it was 500 miles he had to go. He stopped late in the night and dozed for a few minutes with the car idling. He dreamed that he was walking in the woods and that he found Rose frozen solid, sitting up, in a newly fallen bed of snow. He dreamed that it was early in the morning and that he'd come around a corner of the trail and there she was in the middle of the trail, sitting with her head tilted slightly down in the new snow. When he woke up it was an hour before light and when he drove into the city it was chimneys and clothes-lines that stood out now instead of spruce forest against the first light of dawn.

Muskies are for Men

One Friday afternoon on his way home from work Bob Lofgren was killed by a car. It was an especially bad accident: he wasn't even 40 years old, the coach of the local peewee football team and the rugged, gentle, handsome "perfect husband" often cited by his buddies' wives. He had a habit of riding his ten-speed, and he was stopped in the curb lane at an amber light when a Buick going 40 miles an hour hit him from behind. The driver of the Buick was an old man with aluminum crutches and thick eyeglasses, and several months after the accident a story went around the neighbourhood that the old man had died of remorse, but by that time no-one was angry anymore. They all felt sorry for the old man, and they simply felt bad about Susan and little Tom Lofgren, who were minus a husband and father.

An autumn and a winter went by and then spring came, and it was almost a year since the Friday afternoon it happened. Susan Lofgren was a petite woman who walked like a soldier and smiled a lot, even if she didn't feel like it. It was typical of her to volunteer for all sorts of jobs, sometimes even those she couldn't handle, and she had lately decided that if her family no longer had a father she'd have to take on that role herself. So now people would see her sitting with Tom up in the bleachers at the Cubs games or fixing his bike in the back lane or tossing the ball with him out in the front yard, embarrassing him with her funny overhand. This was the summer that Tom would have been old enough to accompany his father on the annual fishing trip to Canada, so Susan Lofgren waited until school was out and then made reservations for the two of them at her husband's old fishing-lodge, a thousand miles to the north.

One bright green early summer morning they slipped out of Chicago and hit the freeway, Canada bound. Tom had spent the last week sorting through his father's collection of northern pike and muskie lures, many of them made by hand, and he had them neatly laid out on the car seat beside him. Some of these lures he'd seen his father make, this tandem bucktail, this tooth-scarred old pine jerk bait. He was thirteen years old, with his mother's fair hair and his father's reticence. Unlike either of them he tended to put on weight easily, on the arms and the legs, like a miniature wrestler, and from the way he wore his baseball cap it was apparent that he took himself quite seriously. Occasionally he would sort through his collection of fishing lures, testing the point of a treble hook on his thumbnail, or solemnly leaf through the stack of fishing magazines while his mother watched out of the corner of her eye, saying, "That's a pretty one," or

37

"What will we catch with that one honey?" while the farmland rolled by and the cornfields turned to hardwood forest and the day wore on.

The second day they crossed the border into Canada and the landscape abruptly changed. Now there was dark virgin forest on both sides of the highway and each time they topped a hill a new lake came into view. In the evening they stopped in a roadside restaurant and Tom pointed to a number of fish that were mounted on the wall. "That's a walleye," he said. "That one there is a smallmouth bass, and that one..." he said, with ominous emphasis, pointing to a dusty old monster with glaring eyes and canine teeth, "that one is a big muskellunge. Or you can call him a muskie, if you want."

His mother made a face. "I wouldn't call him anything. I hope we don't catch any of those, they'll pull us right into the water."

"Mom...a big fish like that, you've got to let him run. That's what your drag is for. Otherwise he'll just break your line."

"I'd rather have him break the line than have him in the boat."

Tom just shook his head. "Mother...you've got to stop thinking like that," he said.

Late that night they arrived at their resort, which was a small hotel several miles off the main highway. The hotel was located right on the river and as they unloaded the car in the parking-lot in the woods it was too dark to see anything but Tom could smell the river.

In the hotel lobby there was no-one in sight. They put down their bags by the vending machines and looked around for a bell. Susan Lofgren heard a strange, snuffling noise and peered into the back room. An old man was tilted back in a cane chair, his back resting against the wall and his head canted forward. With his broad, bony shoulders, fierce nose and bald head he looked like some cartoon buzzard dozing beside a trail. She rapped the door frame smartly and said, "Excuse me?"

The old man coughed out some barely coherent profanity and opened his eyes, then scowled in embarrassment and got to his feet. "Yes ma'am, excuse me, I was resting my eyes for a minute there and I guess I got carried away."

"I'm Susan Lofgren and this is my son Tom, we're from Chicago, and I believe we have reservations?"

The old man was probably less old than weatherbeaten. There were suspenders strapped over his wide shoulder and he had big bony hands. His eyes were fierce and bloodshot and now that he was awake he looked more like a cranky old chicken hawk than a buzzard. "Well...I got some bad news for you, Missus, the guides are all gone on strike, as of yesterday morning, the useless buncha layabouts, and if you're wanting to go fishing you'll have to take a boat out by yourselves."

Her heart sank. "Oh no..." She stared at the wall for a moment. "We can't do that. We've never been here before. We don't know our way around. And besides...it wouldn't be safe. I don't know how to operate a motorboat."

The old man glared down at Tom. "What'sa matter with him? When I was his age I was a licenced guide already. Can't he run the boat for you?"

"I should hope not!" she responded in Tom's defence. "If I can't run a boat how do you suppose he can?"

The man behind the desk glanced darkly at Tom, as if it were all his fault.

Mrs. Lofgren finally spoke. "This is very inconvenient, I don't mind telling you. If it weren't for Tom I'd expect my deposit returned immediately. As it is...I suppose I'll have to operate the blasted motorboat myself, but I'll expect a full set of instructions and a map. And you can tell the manager I'm very annoyed. I realize it's not your fault but I'm sorry, I'm very annoyed."

"Okay, missus, I'll tell him that."

The old man's name was Joe Hudson and he worked from midnight to 6 AM at the hotel desk. At six the manager came in and Joe Hudson went down to the marina and set things up for the little girl who came in at eight. On this particular morning he went down to the marina and saw the boy sitting on the top step.

The boy got up as he rattled his keys. "Good morning, sir," said Tom.

Joe Hudson shot a key into the lock. "You up already boy? Where's your ma?"

"She's still sleeping. I figured I'd do a little fishing off the dock. I figure it's still early, I'd get them while they're biting."

Joe Hudson unlocked the door and they went inside. "You're wasting your time, boy. There's no fish off this dock right now. Walleyes are all in deep water this time of year. Thirty feet or more. You won't get nothing off the end of this dock but perch the size of that chocolate bar."

Tom was carrying a casting rod in one hand and a battered old tackle box in the other. He was wearing a life-jacket buckled to his chin and had the baseball cap snugged down low to his eyes. "Maybe I'd better go catch a few of those perch then.... Are we allowed to fish off the dock?"

"When I was your age we wouldn't waste time fishing for perch. We'd snag big bloody sturgeons and kill 'em with an axe. Then we'd cut them up and sell them to the section gang. We didn't fuss with perch. We'd use hand-lines too. We didn't have expensive outfits like the kids nowadays."

Tom glanced down at the fishing-rod in his hand. "This is my dad's muskie pole."

Joe Hudson took a second look at the boy's rod.

"That rod you got in your hand is older than you and me put together. It might be your dad's rod but it had a lot of owners before him."

"My grandad used to fish muskies in the St. Lawrence

40

river. He used this pole all his life then he passed it to my dad."

Tom handed the rod to Joe Hudson, who scowled as he held it up to the light and examined it. "This here is a hand-made cane pole. You don't see many of these around any more. And I'll tell you something, these are the best rods ever made. I bought one in a big sporting-goods store in New York City when I was down east with the army. Cost me two weeks pay. Had it for 34 years and lost it in a fire. See that flat rock over there on the shoreline? I stood on that flat rock one day and whipped a 48-inch tiger muskie to a standstill. Then I shook off the hook and sent him on his way. A man would never kill a muskie in those days. No more than you'd put a .22 through an eagle."

Tom was looking out the window at the flat rock. "Maybe I should go try a few casts. There could be one sitting out there right now."

Joe Hudson looked at him with a skeptical eye. "How long you here for boy?"

"Four days."

"How would you like to spend your whole four days standing up, casting until your arm aches, and have nothing to show for it?"

Tom responded with a blank look.

"Well that's muskie fishing. You don't take a few casts for muskies. You fish for weeks maybe and you don't even see one. There's only a bit of advice that's worth a damn when it comes to muskie fishing."

Tom nodded.

The old man handed him back his pole. "Quit while you're ahead."

Tom went out to the dock and fished for an hour then went up and had breakfast with his mother. "Did you catch anything Tommy?" she asked.

"I was trying out Dad's muskie rod. The water is really clear and there were lots of minnows following the lure. No muskies though. That grumpy old man was there, and he told me I won't catch anything."

"Don't worry about that. We'll get some fish today."

They went down to the dock and the old man gave them a boat, which they loaded with jackets and picnic box and fishing-gear while he looked on. Finally they were ready to go and Susan Lofgren sat down in the rear of the boat. "Now..." she said, looking nervously at the outboard motor.

"That there is a brand new 25-horsepower motor," he said. "You shouldn't have no trouble with it. You pump the bulb on that hose there, that's right, pump it up tight, then set your throttle to start...yes, that's right, and then pull out that choke button there, that black button, make sure you're in neutral...and now give her a yank."

She stood up, steadied herself with one hand and gave the pull cord a hefty tug. The engine only responded with a loud rude noise and snapped six inches of cord back into the cowling. "I'll have to use both hands," she apologized.

This time she pulled with both hands, and though the engine responded with a more encouraging trio of coughs she almost fell backwards over the boat seat.

"Let me have a look at it," said Joe Hudson, kneeling down. "You got to talk to it."

Her voice was quavering. "Are you sure this motor is operating properly?"

"Well...I'll get it started here, then once it's warmed up it'll start easier for you." He went through the motions of checking the bulb and the choke and the throttle and then fanned the cord with one powerful sweep of his arm, the engine firing immediately and rising to a smooth, fine high-bubbling idle. "There you go," he said. "I marked some good walleye holes on that map. And if you get turned around just flag down a boat and they'll point you the way home."

"Don't worry about us getting lost," she said, "I have no

intention of going out of sight."

Joe Hudson glanced at Tom, whose disappointment at this news was quickly neutralized by his eagerness to get started. "Okay Mom, all ready here," he said.

She shifted into forward and they were off, caroming once off the dock, then barely missing a parked boat and barging slowly out into the open water. Susan Lofgren fed it more and more throttle until they were underway, cruising north-ward at a speed that matched her daring: about twice as fast as a walk.

The day turned brutally hot and quiet. As the morning pro-gressed just a faint gauze of altostratus cloud slowed the relentless hammering of the sun. By noon it was 90 degrees, and no-one in bare feet dared cross the asphalt parking-lot beside the marina. By three in the afternoon it was 95 and even the seagulls had quit for the day, refusing to fly, and floating like littered Javex bottles out on the slack blue skin of the river. At four in the afternoon Mrs. Lofgren and her son motored up and crashed into the dock. Tom scrambled out of the boat and tied the stern and bow while his mother, her face burned shiny and red as a tomato, issued anxious instructions.

The marina girl trotted down to help and Mrs. Lofgren disconnected the gas hose from the motor. "Is this how you stop it?" she asked the girl. "That man, Mr. Hudson, forgot to tell me how to stop it. I've had to listen to this blasted thing all day. The noise and that awful blue smoke, yuck!"

"You push that black rubber button," the girl replied.

Mrs. Lofgren climbed awkwardly out of the boat. "Oh well...I wouldn't have shut it off anyway. I wouldn't want to be stuck out there if I couldn't get it going again."

Tom was wordlessly unloading the boat.

"Did you catch any fish?" the girl asked.

"Well...we had a lovely day. We had a nice boat ride, and we saw some pelicans. I think we caught two fish, what

43

were they Tom? A perch and a rock bass? Tom knows all the types of fish, you know. He's got a big aquarium at home and he sends away for all the fishing magazines. I think he caught the bug from his father."

Tom picked up his gear and looked at the girl. "Two crummy little panfish."

"Well Tom!" his mother scolded lightly. "You needn't insult my two little fish. They're the only fish we saw all day. If you'd try something besides those big silly-looking wooden lures we might have caught enough for supper."

That night Mrs. Lofgren curled up in the hotel-room with an old Clark Gable movie on the television but Tom didn't want to be there. He sat at the end of the dock and batted mosquitoes in the dusk and then he went up and visited Joe Hudson in the hotel lobby. Joe Hudson ignored him at first but then he started talking, suspiciously watching Tom anyway, as if he were afraid Tom was going to take something away from him. He told Tom about growing up in the bush, on the trapline, about the time he was a little boy in his mother's arms on the dogsled and the wolves were chasing them and his old man was tumbling them with the carbine. He told Tom about growing up and going to war, learning to smoke cigarettes, throwing a grenade into a farmhouse window in Normandy and killing seventeen German soldiers and a dog. He told Tom about working as a fishing-guide, bringing in a six-pound walleye one day and feeling a bump on the line and seeing nothing left of the walleye but a severed head. Tom went to bed that night dreaming of misty forgotten bays where muskies as big as alligators lurked just beneath the surface.

The next day there was a thunderstorm at daybreak, and by breakfast time it had settled into an all-day drizzling rain. Tom stood dolefully at the door of the marina, studying the sky for any sign of a letup, while Joe Hudson sat smoking his pipe, his thumb hooked smugly in his suspender, and judged that it would rain like hell until evening. "You might just as well go hunting for a pile of comic books," Joe Hudson declared. "Your ma is a woman and I've yet to see a woman go fishing in the rain."

Tom and his mother had breakfast and then she went shopping in town. He put on a suit of yellow rain gear and spent the day at the end of the dock, one rod rigged with a bobber and a worm, the other rod, his cane muskie pole, hung with a triple bucktail spinner with which he tirelessly flogged the river. The only occurrence of any note was a curious bulge in the water that followed his lure three times in a row. Each time, as his bucktail swam in toward him, he tried to catch a glimpse of the pursuer but the water was as blank and shiny as aluminum. That evening he told Joe Hudson about the bulge in the water and Joe Hudson lifted an eyebrow and stared. "That's a follow," he said. "You got followed by something."

Joe Hudson went to the window and squinted out into the darkness and rain. "If it stops raining I'll take you and your ma out fishing in the morning," he said.

But it kept on raining and got colder instead. All day long Tom stood on the slippery boards of the dock and threw muskie lures at the river. His hands were numb and his legs were stiff from standing in one position all day and when his mother finally came down to get him for supper he felt like crawling into a cupboard somewhere and closing the door. Tomorrow night they were going home and he hadn't caught a fish yet, not one single fish. Even the little perch stayed away from his hook, as if they knew how happy it would make him if he even caught one of them. He'd be famous at his school, the guy who went to the Canadian wilderness and never caught a fish. It made him feel so lousy he couldn't speak.

In the morning the rain had stopped and the sky was full of big soggy clouds. Joe Hudson met them down at the dock and predicted sunshine by noon, but Tom was beginning to realize that Joe Hudson didn't know much more about the weather than the guy on the radio did. They got in the boat and five minutes later they were cruising wide-open on the river. In no time they passed the reef that marked the outer limit he and his mother explored, and then it was real wilderness, no cabins, no boats, just chains of islands going by, and high cliffs battened with mist. The river was as grey as a highway and the air was cold. His mother was trying to cheer him up again, as usual, and Tom sat a foot away from her with his cap pulled down low, nodding whenever she pointed to where a diving duck or osprey skimmed down and zippered open the perfect mirror image of the river. Finally they went up into a narrow canyon where the river seemed to bulge and simmer with power. Joe Hudson slowed the boat and turned it around. The water was flowing by quite briskly on both sides but when Tom looked at the shore he could see that they were just standing still in the current.

Mrs. Lofgren unbuttoned her jacket. "This is a lovely spot. Tom...do you see where the swallows have built their mud nests up among those rocks?"

Tom was busy with his fishing-tackle. He had the cane muskie rod across his knees and he was tying on a modified Rampage. "Is this a muskie spot or a walleye spot?" he asked.

Joe Hudson frowned. "This is a walleye spot. Don't you want to catch some lunch? Or would you prefer to throw that hardware all morning and then have Spam sandwiches."

Tom shrugged offhandedly and reached for his little spinning-rod. "I'd like to try fishing for walleyes...if you think we'll catch one."

"Of course we'll catch some," his mother said. "We've got the best guide in the area, don't we? Remember what that waitress told us about Mr. Hudson, Tom? Besides...we have to catch some fish or we'll go hungry. Just like the cavemen days."

Tom snapped a black jig onto his line and flipped it out

46

into the current. Joe Hudson threaded a fat night crawler onto Mrs. Lofgren's hook while she averted her eyes and quickly lowered it into the water. Then he set up his own line with a night crawler and fed it into the river. "This is a guaranteed walleye hole," he said. "When I was a boy we'd come here and fill a burlap sack until you couldn't lift it out of the boat."

"Would your guests ever get angry if they had to eat Spam for lunch?" Mrs. Lofgren asked.

Joe Hudson sniffed. "We always caught fish. I never cooked Spam in my life."

They had lunch on a small island off the main channel. There was a grove of eastern Whites on the island and the ground was springy with moss and brown needles. Joe Hudson built a fire of birch bark and pine needles while Mrs. Lofgren sliced the onions and potatoes. Joe Hudson greased a skillet and laid it down on the curling orange flames, then opened his Buck knife and began peeling thin slices from the block of Spam.

Tom went down and sat on a boulder beside the river. Several minutes later his mother came down. "Tom, there will be some food ready in a minute. You better come up and have something to eat."

"No thanks," he said. I'm not eating that stuff, he thought to himself.

"Try to see the positive side," she said. "It's such a nice island, and I think the sun is going to come out. Why don't you come up and sit with us? Nobody really cares if we caught any fish or not."

He looked away from her. He had to, he was so depressed. It was easy for her to look on the positive side, she didn't care about fishing in the first place. She treated it like a dumb little game, like when she'd go to the hockey game and clap for both sides. If she'd just stop trying to act like his father this wouldn't have happened. He was always get-

47

ting his hopes up, then she'd turn back into his mother and the whole thing would fall apart in his lap...it was so embarrassing in front of everybody.

"Maybe next year we'll have better luck," she said. "Mr. Hudson says he'll take us out again."

"I don't want to come back next year," Tom replied.

She looked at him for several moments before answering. "Do you mean you're going to give up fishing? What about your grandad's muskie rod? You take such good care..."

"I didn't say I was going to give up fishing," Tom replied. "I just don't want to go any more with you."

His mother sat down on her heels and pulled at a small flower that was growing in the rocks. After a while she was crying. "I want to tell you something," she sniffed. "We both lost somebody a year ago...and now we don't have anybody to take care of us anymore. I take you to baseball games, I take you on fishing trips and you just get mad at me. Do you think I like to sleep on hard beds and get bitten by mosquitoes? I'm doing this for you! And so is Mr. Hudson there...he's been up all night working, and now he's putting himself out for your sake, hoping you might catch a big fish. And you've never once smiled or even said thank you."

She shook her head and attempted to stare at him angrily, but her eyes were too full of water. She mopped her eyes with a Kleenex and stood up to leave. "I tried so hard for you, Tom," she said "but it just wasn't good enough, was it? So next year I really don't want to go fishing with you either."

All the way back to the lodge they cruised at half-speed and stopped to cast at various weed beds and reefs. Susan Lofgren, veteran actress that she was, wore owlish sunglasses over her reddened eyes and added chuckles and comments to Joe Hudson's narrative. By late afternoon the sun was out and putting heat on the river. There was bird song rattling in the woods and marine life visible in the jade-green transparent water. "These three-day blows always wreck the fishing," Joe Hudson said. He looked like a bug-eyed turtle stretching his neck out of the loose folds of underwear. "But damn, it's nice to feel that sun."

They were backing in a large circle around a large underwater stone pile, while Tom and his mother worked the water with surface lures. There were clumps of cabbage weed growing up between the boulders and Joe Hudson was navigating a slow passage in reverse. Then suddenly he lifted his arm and pointed almost angrily. "There's your muskie," he said.

Tom looked across the water and saw the rings where something had come to the surface. he'd never seen any disturbance in his life like this one though, a swirling roll as wide as a kitchen table. Joe Hudson shook his finger. "Cast."

"What is it?" asked Tom's mother.

Tom took her shoulder and pointed her in the right direction. "Mom...look! It's a muskie! Take a cast at it."

Joe Hudson sounded even angrier. "Cast! He's got to hit it right away or not at all."

Mrs. Lofgren's lure flew out and hit the water fifteen feet from the centre of the swirl. Tom's lure was still coming down through the air when the muskellunge surfaced and smashed his mother's lure and almost knocked the rod out of her hands. She cried out in alarm and pulled back and the fish came head and shoulders out of the water and porpoised sideways, his head shaking back and forth as if in violent denial and his red gills flared wide and the water spray flying. Then the line cut down into the water and the fish was diving, digging for the deep water. Tom and Joe Hudson shouted advice and Joe Hudson was gunning the motor in reverse, edging toward the same deep water that the fish had erred in choosing. As the boat followed the muskie a slackening in line pressure turned the fish and he came speeding back toward the boat as if to ram it broadside but broke off the charge at the last second and dug hard with its tail and came clear out of the water like he'd been shot from a gun, and just hung there, perfect, so close that when he hit the water coming down it sprayed the boat.

Now they'd really drifted into the deep water and the fish seemed to calm down with the extra distance from the boat. He was down there, like a dead weight, and as long as Mrs. Lofgren didn't anger him he seemed willing to swim at the end of this long line. They floated for five minutes this way, while Tom and Joe Hudson anxiously coached her, and she concentrated on letting her heart settle down. The fish was uncomfortable and made small concessions as they drifted, and she exploited these, one after the other, until the fish finally lost its temper and went on another rampage, and tired itself further, and gave up a little more.

Finally it came to the surface only twenty feet away and swam, like a leashed dog, in a wide circle around the boat. Tom was slapping her on the back and jumping up and down and Joe Hudson was beaming a gap-toothed grin, brandishing the net. She looked at the guide and at her son, and she looked for a long minute at the fish, which was glassy-eyed and bulldog-jawed but obviously growing more feeble in its attempts to stay away from the boat. It was so unfair, what they were doing to it. She looked at Joe Hudson. "We don't have to kill it, do we?"

Joe Hudson cocked an eyebrow, looked at Tom.

Tom looked at his mother. "My vote is, let it go. That's what Dad always did."

"It's bad luck to kill your first muskie, missus," Joe Hudson said. "You can come back next year and get one for the wall."

"Oh good," she said cheerfully, "I'll do that instead."

For four days Tom had carried a pair of pliers on his belt and now at last he got to use them. Joe Hudson prepared to grab the line at the leader but he saw that Tom was already on his knees, reaching for the fish. "How big is he Mr. Hudson?"

"He's about 45 inches long, weighs 28 pounds, I'd guess. That's a helluva nice fish."

"Look Mom," Tom said, removing the hook in one easy motion from the fish's chin. "If he'd jumped one more time it would have fallen out."

Tom was holding the muskie with both hands around its midsection, marvelling at its fierce eyes, its docility, the blue and green iridescence of its scales. Joe Hudson and his mother leaned on the gunwhale of the boat and watched as Tom removed his hands and the fish gave a tired sweep of the tail and they all gave a little cheer as it slowly swam back down into the shadows from which it came.

Tom made a special point this evening of meeting all the other fishing boats when they came in, just so that he could ask them how fishing was, then accidentally mention that his mother, yep, that lady right over there, caught a real nice 28-pound muskie this afternoon, which they released just like they always do, being the good sports that they are. Then they went up and had dinner and re-fought the fish for everyone's benefit six or eight times, and the hotel manager came by and congratulated them. And by that time it was 8 PM on a lovely warm summer evening and they decided to put off their departure until first thing in the morning, and maybe go out casting for an hour, now that they'd finally clicked.

Joe Hudson walked down to the dock with Tom, intending to say goodbye to Mrs. Lofgren, and once again they found her engaged in a dire wrestling match with the outboard motor. Tom and Joe Hudson watched silently while the engine spat and coughed and fought back, then Tom tapped his mother on the shoulder. "Mother...do you want me to try it?"

His mother looked quizzically at him for a moment and

then moved out of his way. Tom stepped down into the boat and yanked the pull-cord and the motor started. The baseball cap was pulled low and business-like over his eyes and he was wearing his pliers and his one leather glove. He looked up at Joe Hudson. He didn't say anything.

"I'd come with you but I got to get some sleep before work," Joe Hudson said. "But I've never seen a prettier evening for throwing lures. Don't forget to try that weed line I told you about."

"I won't forget."

"Are you sure you don't want me to drive, Tom?" his mother asked. "Then you can concentrate on your fishing."

Tom waved goodbye to Joe Hudson and slowly powered the boat away from the dock. "I'll drive for now, Mother. We'll just work it out as we go along."

Tourist Season

Sitting behind the wheel of this big Winnebago motor-home Frank shifted the cigar from one side of his mouth to the other and glanced at me, as I was staring out the window. "Seen any seals yet, kid?"

I shook my head. "Not a one."

I was beginning to suspect that Frank was putting me on. He'd told me that there were going to be seals in the water alongside the highway, once we got into Canada, but I'd been watching the scenery for over an hour now and it didn't look much different from the Minnesota side. We were into hilly country now, up and down, up and down. There was forest on both sides of the road, rocky ridges and an endless series of swamps and lakes. We'd driven all night through sleepy Wisconsin townships and upstate Minnesota iron range. The big trucks idling at the roadhouses had been covered with red dust. All the cars and even the people had red dust on them, and then sometime after midnight we crossed the border. Around four in the morning Frank pulled over and parked for a few hours and we slept. At day-break we woke up surrounded by mist. Inside the camper guys were farting and snoring, and I went outside. I felt dead after too much whisky and not enough sleep. Steve was up already. He was standing outside in the mist, taking a leak on the cinders. "Where are we?" I said. Outside it was all rocks and trees and mist. Weird cries of birds.

Steve looked around. "Fog city," he said. "I dunno. Maybe we died and went to heaven."

Half-hour later we were rolling again. Naturally we get right back into the hooch, hangover remedy. Then Frank tells me to watch for seals in the lakes, because we're pretty far north now. Frank can tell you anything, and you'd prob-ably believe him. He's got a hell of a sales ability. He owns the little door-and-window company I work for in Milwaukee. Also, he's my uncle. I'm still keeping an eye out for seals when we pull into Frank's top-secret fishing-spot, this grubby little backwoods town called Keewuttunnee. I'm a little annoyed when later that night one of the locals tells me there's no seals for a thousand miles. Frank and the other guys just point their fingers and laugh at me. "It's your own fault, kid. You believed us." I realize that I better be on my toes or they won't give me a minute's rest.

But that's getting ahead of the story. When we get to Keewuttunnee we check into this fleabag hotel, the Bay Inn. Then we grab a few hours sleep. Then we head down and have a few cool ones in the beer parlour. That's what they're called in Canada, "beer parlours." You aren't supposed to have a good time in there. You're just supposed to sit in your chair and swallow that ale. That doesn't slow the guys down though. They're strolling all over the bar and making friends like they're at a house party. Frank seems to know everyone's name but nobody knows Frank from a hole in the ground. These locals up in Canada must all be inbred, Ozark hillbillies. This one guy, Burt Harrison, keeps telling us he's going to have one more drink and then "take the whole shebang." Nobody knows what the hell he's talking about. Dumb as a sackful of rocks.

Around eight o'clock we go into the dining-room and order dinner. Our waitress comes out. An Indian girl and man, she's a beauty. Long black hair, big eyes and this willowy set of pins you can't stop looking at. I've never seen anything like her. She looks just like that Cheyenne princess in *Jeremiah Johnson*. I guess she notices me staring at her because she gives me a little smile. We eat dinner. By now the rest of the guys have noticed her too and they're starting to have a good time. When she brings our bill Burt takes her by the hand. "Honey, what's your name?"

She pulls her hand back and struts into the kitchen, throwing her hair behind her in an angry little snap. The boys laugh. They think this is funny as hell. Burt turns over the tab and reads the back of it. "Thank you. Come again. Diana."

More laughter. "Come again," Frank says, slapping his knee.

Steve sips at his beer. "That's what a girl said to me at a party the other night."

No matter what you say to Steve on a fishing-trip he always has the same answer: that's what a girl said to me at a party the other night. Hey Steve, can I have some? Hey Steve, your rod is jerking. Wow Steve, it looks like a big one...That's what a girl said to me at a party the other night. After dinner the guys leave a big tip for Diana. They're the kind of guys that think you can say whatever you want to a waitress as long as you leave a nice big tip. Maybe they're right, because the next morning she's nice and cool and pleasant as she waits on us. Maybe she gets this treatment from all the tourists, or maybe Indian girls are so cool, from living in tune with Nature, that normal hassles just don't affect them. Whatever, she seems to know that I'm watching her. As we're leaving to go fishing, she gives me a nice little glance, a smile. I guess she can tell I'm a fan. I'm a married man at the time, so I'm not trying to hustle her. I just think she's neat.

I'm a rookie on this trip, first time I've been fishing in my life, so Frank explains to me that you've gotta draw lots for guides. Me and Steve are in the same boat together because we're both new boys, and the guide who takes us out knows even less about fishing than I do. He takes us to a place where the water's about three feet deep and then he starts into this long conversation with Steve about rock concerts. Meanwhile I'm sitting there with my hook hanging in the water hoping that maybe some fish will come by and snag his nose on it. Frank and Nick have this young Indian guy with them and he's obviously all-pro. Every time they go by the Indian guy is standing up in the back of the boat real casual with his foot up on the seat like it's a park bench instead of an aluminum boat tearing along at 30 miles an hour and Frank and Nick are both grinning, waving to us and holding their hands apart to show us how big the fish was. At lunch they've got so many on their stringer—great big damned walleyes—that their guide Sonny can barely lift them out of the boat. Wally and Burt have this old geezer named Joe Hudson for a guide but at least they've caught some fish. Me and Steve, we've got these two little tiny ones that are worse than nothing, they're so puny in comparison. Next day it's the same thing. We get this same bozo for a guide and once again me and Steve are pretty well skunked at shore-lunch, while the rest of the guys have caught all these nice fish. Third day, same thing. I've gotta sit in the boat all day with Steve, who's useless as tits on a bull, and this so-called guide, who laughs like hell every time I try to say something to Steve and Steve says, "That's what a girl said to me at a party the other night." The whole arrangement is fixed, I'm beginning to realize. This daily draw is fixed. This numbskull guide is either being paid off or he's got a rare talent for screwing up, and it's clear that there's not a damned thing I can do about it. As far as Frank and the rest of the older guys are concerned this guide doesn't make any difference anyway. They bring back all the fish because they're more *skillful,* you see. At shore-lunch they spend the whole time laughing at me and Steve and showing us what a fish looks like. They tell us there's no extra fish for lunch but if we ask them real nice they'll sell us a couple. One day we're sitting out there and Steve is snoozing in the bottom of the boat and I'm fishing and the guide is staring at his shoelace when Frank and Nick pull up in their boat with Sonny Copenace and they stand up and start throwing fish at us, live walleyes, big ones too, and we have to duck as these big fish come flying over and splash into the water around us and then Sonny hits the throttle and they go roaring away. This is real funny, of course. I've been sitting here trying to catch just *one* fish like the ones that are flying past my head. I'm starting to think about all the Thursday nights we've gone for drinks at the Five Points and they've put salt in my beer or buried a sulphur match in one of my cigarettes when I'm in the can. I'm starting to think of all the nice little girls like Diana that they've scared half to death by telling them that the guy over at the shuffleboard, the guy that just said something nice to her and bought her a drink (me) is awaiting trial for gross buggery offences or something. I'm starting to think of all the other things I could be doing this week, instead of stumbling around the backwoods of Canada providing these guys with comic relief.

Every night the regular deal was to go into the bar and sit

around. After a few nights of that I got to the point where I'd just have one beer and then truck off to my room and watch TV. The guys would always wave at me and say goodnight in falsetto voices and send their love to my teddy bear. One night I was in the hotel lobby browsing through the magazine stand when the big swinging door from the dining-room opened and somebody walked past me. I had my nose in the magazine.

"Oh...hi," she says.

I turned around and there she was, standing there in her snug designer blue jeans and windbreaker with the purse over her shoulder. She's got a little Indian choker around her neck and a flower in her hair. She's standing there motionless with her eyes big and slightly startled. I nod to her without smiling. "Hello Diana...you all through work for another night?"

She nods. "Yes."

"You never go in the bar after work?"

"I'm not old enough."

"Uh-huh... Well don't feel bad. You're not missing much."

She walks to the magazine stand and looks down the row of books, touches a fashion magazine. She opens it and flips through the pages. Girls with spiky hair and expressions like vampires. She'd told me she's underage, now she's got to show me how sophisticated she is. I'm surprised, because that's just what a girl from Milwaukee would do. Diana glances at me over the corner of the magazine. "Don't you go in the bar with your friends?"

"Well...they're not really my friends. They're just a bunch of guys I work with. The company sponsors a fishing-trip every year."

She nods.

I flip through the pages of my magazine. Diana flips through the pages of hers. Finally she puts it back on the rack. She gives the shoulder strap of her purse a little hitch.

58

"I guess…"

I stick my magazine back in its place. If I hadn't waited until now she might have said no. "Can I walk you home?"

She looks at me. Am I really as trustworthy as I let on? I guess she can see that I'm just curious, I'm not really trying to hustle her. She gives me that little smile. "Okay."

On the way home she laughs, because I'm asking her so many questions. She seems a little shy. Once you get her talking, though, you've really pulled the cork out of a bottle. She tells me all about this little town she lives in. She tells me about her family. Her dad died last year. She's got no boyfriends but Sonny Copenace likes her. She's worked at the hotel since May, when she got out of the Youth Centre. Elsie Hudson is a nice lady. She manages the hotel and she lives in that house right over there. We walk on through the town in the dark with the dogs barking and the drone of a boat way out there lonely in the dark on the river and there are no streetlights so the millions of stars are spread overhead so close they're almost scary, you keep looking up at them. Diana tells me about Stan Highway her older brother and Eddie her younger brother who she never got to know because he died in a boat accident with her mother quite a few years back. Then another time, when her dad had quit drinking, John Murphy who is a cop brought a bottle past the house and said, I'll give you a jug of Gold Tassel for that cross fox and her dad drank the bottle and fell down the stairs and broke his hip, and that's why Diana had to go to the Youth Centre, because she went over to the town side and took out the windows on John Murphy's cop car with one of Stan's hockey sticks.

Then we cross an old steel trestle bridge with a big emptiness underneath, somewhere down there is the river we go fishing on in the morning, then down some mud roads between rows of dark shabby old houses, Indian reserve. I'm really learning a few things tonight. About two hundred yards from the end of the road she tells me we better stop.

59

Down there is her brother Stan's house, where she's been staying. I better not walk her to the door in case Sonny is visiting. We stand there for a few minutes. I give her a cigarette and she smokes it awkwardly, not inhaling. We look up at the stars. A little green meteorite loops across the star bed. She says, "That means the end of the world is coming." I haven't said a thing about my wife, and when she finally comes right out and asks me I just say no, I'm not married. I sure don't feel married, either. Four days in the bush and I've forgotten all my obligations already. That's the kind of guy I was.

So Diana gives me a little kiss on the cheek as I'm leaving. This cheers me up a bit. If nothing else she sure is good looking.

At breakfast Diana waits on our table but I don't say anything about the night before. It's funny, but these older guys are hard to predict. One minute they're making dirty jokes about some girl; the next they're being all protective about her like she's their daughter. They've been away from their wives for a few days now so Diana has sort of become their number one girl. If one of the guys has a new joke he tries it out on her. If she doesn't get the double-meaning part they all laugh like hell. Nick has gotten onto this old song and now the other guys are singing it too. It's becoming this trip's theme song.

You're so young and I'm so old
This my darling I am told
But oh, please, stay with me...Diana

Very funny. When Diana comes out carrying the breakfast tray usually somebody only has to sing the first line of the song to get a laugh. It's a regular part of the meal. That's why I don't want to say anything about the night before. I get enough grief from these guys already without declaring open warfare by stealing their girl. After breakfast I kill a few minutes in the washroom while the other guys go down to the boats. Then I have a quick accidental conversation with Diana. Can I meet you after work tonight? She nods her head really quick like she's been hoping that I would ask her that. There's something about being close to her like this, I don't know. I've got a rocket in my pants as I go running down to the boats.

At shore-lunch I'm loading my plate, famished, last in line, daydreaming about tonight, and Frank sneaks up behind me and ties a nylon stringer to my belt loop. A nylon stringer is a cord, you see, about five feet long. He ties the other end to a tree. Meanwhile I'm thinking about me, Diana and a green bed of moss out in the forest. When I'm all finished loading my plate, buttering my bread, squeezing lemon juice on the fish, salt and peppering my potatoes, I turn to walk away and I hit the end of the cord and drop my lunch all over the ground. There's a roar of laughter you can probably hear all the way to Keewuttunnee. I don't say anything, even though it's all I can do to keep from breaking Frank's face. I just get down on the ground and pick up the scattered pieces of my lunch, brush off the twigs and bits of rock. I'm going to get you bastards, if it's the last thing I do.

By three in the afternoon it's clouded over and blowing. By four o'clock it's raining like a cow pissing on a flat rock and we're running up to the cabins with tackle boxes and beer coolers in hand. God doesn't seem to be co-operating with my plan to spawn with Diana in the wild woods. That night it's dinner and then into the bar, as usual. Two young guys from Winnipeg join the boys at the table and everyone's bullshitting and tossing back the beer. Frank and Nick start jabbering like monkeys when they find out that these guys have some marijuana. They've just discovered dope, you see. There's nothing they like better than to sneak into the can at the Five Points and smoke up a reefer they scored from some fourteen-year-old who's probably in school with their sons. But they can't smoke up here, that's obvious. The two Canadians say, well, let's go out to our cottage for a party. Fine, great idea. Going to a stag party with all these guys appeals to me abut as much as gargling Drano so I say goodnight. I'm quite depressed. It's still drizzling outside. Diana will be off work soon and there's nowhere to go. She's too young for the bar and Sonny Copenace will scalp me if we go back to her house. We can't go up to my hotel-room because she works here and she'd balk at that. Can't blame her. So much for my one shot at the big time. I wait in line at the pay phone with the other turistas, waiting to place the regular nightly phone call to the wife. She tells me that the Audi won't start. Probably the ignition relay that keeps corroding in damp weather and has cost me a small fortune already. Sell the godamned rattletrap. Irene Webster is expecting again and the paper boy still won't put the paper in between the doors. Have you caught any fish? I'm standing there talking to her when Nick comes inside with his raincoat all slick. He trots upstairs to get a bottle. Outside in the parking-lot I can see the Winnebago, its parking lights winking in the rain. I'm hearing about the Mutual Bank's weird letter about our mortgage when Diana comes out of the dining-room, slinging the strap of her purse over her shoulder. She stands at the window, looking hesitantly out at the rain when I cup my hand over the phone and call to her. "Diana...wait a minute."

Sometimes I wonder what I'd be doing today if she hadn't chosen that moment to walk by.

The guys are shocked as hell when I come out with Diana and announce that we're joining them to go to the party. We all pile onto the bus. The two Canadian guys are looking at me like I'm crazy. Nick guns the big motor-home up the hill and around the corner and through the wet little town. It's dark inside the camper; everybody's drinking beer and cracking jokes. Diana is sitting beside me on the couch seat in the very back and I've got my arm around her and I can

smell the little flower in her hair. In the crawling shadow
light I can see glimpses of the guys as they look over at me,
and though they're glad Diana's coming along they're not
too overjoyed to see me sitting there with my arm around
her. Steve is so excited that our patron saint goddess is on
the bus with us he's practically incoherent. What does he
think is going to happen? I ask myself. No matter what,
there sure won't be any extra for him. Frank is wearing a big
smile but there's that little nervous stitch in his eyebrow,
the same one he wears when he's playing poker riding a big
bet with a dick hand. A few miles out of town we turn off
the highway and onto this little bush road. We drive slow
down the road with pine branches slapping the windows.
One of the Canadians yells at Nick to watch for a white
board nailed to a tree with Taylor on it. Pretty soon we stop
and we're there. Everyone piles out. We go into the cottage
and the owner of the place gets a fire going and his buddy
puts on the stereo. One of them produces a big fat reefer and
it starts making the rounds. Diana sits on the couch and
Nick and Frank and Steve sit around her and I can hear Nick
asking her if she's planning to go to university and
meanwhile I've got the rye and coke and I'm mixing her a
big tall glass of panty remover. We all sort of relax and party
for about 45 minutes and Diana drains the whole glass of
liquor. She's about half-way through her second one and
Frank even has his arm sort of sprawled along the back of the
couch behind her like a kid at a drive-in when I saunter up
and take her by the hand and she stands up automatically,
like she's hypnotized. Frank looks up at me with a sick look
on his face. "Where you going?"

I don't say anything. I just wink at him. Revenge is
sweet. "Do you think Diana and I have nothing better to do
than sit around and listen to you guys b.s. all night?"

Frank looked at Steve. "Where's he going?"

I had my arm around Diana's waist and we were heading
for the door.

"I think we've been had," Nick remarked.

I can still imagine the scene. The party in decline. Glum envious faces. Every once in a while a face coming to the door and peeking out. Barely audible sounds coming from the camper. Black trees. Wisconsin licence plates. Falling rain.

The next day the guys were kind of in awe of me. I guess they'd learned their lesson. Frank and Nick offered to let us go out with Sonny Copenace, since it was the last day of the trip and we hadn't really caught any fish yet. Right off the bat I hooked into a huge bloody northern pike that took fifteen minutes to get in the boat. We dragged it out of the boat at shore-lunch and everybody gasped. At nineteen pounds it was easily the biggest fish caught all week. Everybody stood around taking pictures of themselves with my fish. Nick told me to sit down and he brought me a drink. "Here, rookie," he said. Him and Frank had been out with Johnny NoCash all morning and they hadn't caught a thing. I kept asking them what had happened. They didn't have any smart answers for a change. I could have really rubbed it in but I was starting to get a little bit tired of all this tit-for-tat nonsense. Truth is, I felt better right then than I had in a long time. Good sunlight shining down. Good clean rocky land. I was thinking about sweet Diana constantly, lonesome for her and we hadn't even left yet. I found a nice soft place on the moss and stretched out for a few minutes, pulled the baseball cap down over my eyes. I could hear Frank telling everybody how we'd fish until five, have dinner, pack up and try and be on the road by eight. Somebody sat down on the moss beside me. I cocked open one eye and saw that it was Johnny NoCash. He sat there not saying anything, eating his lunch. Guides always eat last, you see. Finally he put his plate down and leaned back and fired up a cigarette. When he spoke it was real quiet and low, like he didn't want the other guys to hear him. "You were messing around with Diana Highway last night?"

"Nope," I said, quick as a wink. Then I think to myself, what am I lying to him for? I'm not ashamed of what I did. Hell, that girl Diana, she's worth any six of us.

He spits out a little fleck of tobacco and smiles. "Hey... don't get me wrong. I don't blame you. I've given her a tumble once or twice myself."

"Oh yeah?" Sure you did, slime, I think to myself.

He shrugs. "Well sure. Just a few weeks ago, as a matter of fact. Half the guys in town have been jumpin' on her."

I guess he can see the surprise written on my face because he looks at me and laughs. "Don't tell me you thought you were getting special privileges."

Damnit. That girl deserves an Oscar. It took most of an hour to talk her out of her jeans. Johnny NoCash takes a long slow lazy draw on his cigarette and looks at me. He blows the smoke out. "That's the good news."

"What do you mean."

He looks out at the lake, kind of sad. "Think of the worst possible thing I could tell you right now."

I'm silent for a long minute. Then I look at him. "You don't mean..."

He just nods. "She's carrying the clap."

The rest of the afternoon is like a funeral to me. At four o'clock the rain arrives right on time and we end our fishing-trip running home in a squall. Back at the hotel I'm sitting on the bed soaked to the skin shivering and feeling like I wish somebody would come in and put a bullet through my head. What am I going to tell my wife? How am I going to explain to her that I can't touch her for the next two weeks? What if it turns out to be some exotic Canadian strain that they haven't found a cure for yet? It's Galloping Indian Jungle-Rot, son, I'm afraid your future isn't going to be pleasant. Why was I such a fool? Why didn't I listen to Frank's advice? I keep dropping my trousers and standing in front of the mirror to check the equipment, which looks normal so far, invisible in its early stages as the worst diseases usually are. I made the mistake of telling Steve the bad news and now of course everybody from the hotel bartender down to the goddamn dock boy probably knows that I slept with Diana Highway the night before and picked up a dose. Nick and Frank and Steve and Wally and Burt seem to be handling the news well, if the sound of them gasping, hooting and wretching with laughter in the room down at the end of the hall is any indication. At supper-time I stay cloistered in my room, biting my nails and really starting to regret ever having come on this trip. This quite possibly could be the major error of my life. If my wife finds out, god, I can't even imagine what will happen. Every once in a while I can hear a roar of laughter down in the dining-room and I can only imagine too well what they're talking about. Finally I pack up my duffel bag and my fishing-gear. I take the back exit down to the parking-lot. I'm afraid that if I see Diana I'll lose my temper and smack her or something.

I'm out in the Winnebago, storing the gear under the couch seat in the back when I look out the window and see Diana coming. She's just wearing her little hostess outfit and she's running awkward on her high heels with her head uncovered in the rain. She knocks at the front door of the motor-home. I open it a bit but not so that she can come in. What do you want?

She tells me my dinner is getting cold. It's sitting there on the table. What's the matter? Did I get sick when I was out fishing?

"You should know who's sick," I say to her. "Half this town is sick because of you. Don't you have any shame? Don't you have any decency?"

She steps back a bit, surprised that I've found out. Her eyes darken and her lips begins to tremble. She tries the sympathy bit. What, she says. Is something wrong?

My manner is offhand, as it always is when I'm angry.

Bitch, I say to her. You know very well what's wrong. If you're going to screw every man that comes along you could at least get yourself a shot of penicillin once in a while. Don't you care that I've got a decent wife back home?

Her left eyebrow narrows down a bit. She props a hand on her hip. "You told me you weren't married."

Now she's going to act like I'm more in the wrong than her, an old female trick. I climb out of the Winnebago and slam the door. I glance at her as I'm walking away. "So I lied."

She trots after me. "Who were you talking to?"

I smile at her. "Everybody, Diana... Everybody knows you're a little slut."

That does it. She starts smacking me on the back of the head. It feels like little bursts of wind, frantic moth wings. I duck into the side door of the hotel ahead of her and pull the door shut behind me. I give the panic bar a yank so that she's locked out. Of course the first thing she does is scream and start banging on the door with her little fists. I turn around and give her one half of the peace sign. The rain has messed her hair and she's standing their beating on the glass like a blackbird in a bottle. I stand there with my finger pointing at the ceiling. Absorb the message, sweetheart. She bends down and picks up a handful of cinders and flings them at the glass. I smile at her, you missed. She kicks the door and her face screws up in pain. She starts casting her eyes around on the ground as if she's looking for a rock. She finds a little stick and jams it into the crack between the doors, as if she's going to pry them open. I go back up to my room, after giving her one last rude salute. A minute or two later I hear a window break downstairs, then the manager's voice angry as hell. Five minutes later there's a cop car sitting out on the lawn with its flasher blinking.

So long Diana. I owe you one.

You'd think that was the end of it but no, of course not. Things are bad, but before they get better they're going to get worse. I feel horrible, dirty as a trash can. We've paid off the hotel guy and packed up the Winnebago and now it's almost dark, still raining, miserable goddamn cold night, and we've said our goodbyes and we're on our way home. Nick is taking the first shift at the wheel. I'm in the back seat, feeling sorry for myself. I'm watching the stupid ugly little houses of Keewuttunnee go swaying by when an old red Dodge pickup goes chopping past us then suddenly slows down and pulls in front of us. Frank spills his beer. "Damnit! What the—?"

The truck is parked in front of us with the turn signal flashing. The door opens and Sonny Copenace piles out. Nick turns to Steve. "Did you give him his tip."

"Of course I did."

Wally is the quietest guy among us but he can also smell trouble a mile away. "We got an unhappy Indian on our hands," Wally says, putting his beer down careful so it won't spill.

Sonny walks with that loose-hipped saunter of his up to the front door of the bus and yanks at the handle. Nothing happens. He puts both hands on his hips and looks down the road a bit. His mouth is kind of open and his hair is tied back in the pigtail and he looks like Cochise or somebody. You've got to know this guy Sonny. He's a strong dude but it takes a lot to get him riled. He turns back to the door and there's a loud bang. I guess he's kicked us. "Open up," he shouts.

"This is bullshit," says Wally quietly. He stands up and moves to the front of the bus. Wally is an ex-marine and this kind of thing is his specialty. He opens the door and steps down and looks at the place on the door where Sonny kicked it. He's shaking his head a little bit. It's raining quite hard and Wally is just wearing this blue polo shirt.

"What did you guys do to Diana," Sonny says, clenching and un-clenching his fists as he looks at Wally. Sonny has shoulders like a monkey and you can see he's fixing to unload

68

on Wally. "The cops have her. What did you guys do to her?"

Wally is still checking the door. "You kicked my door, right here." Wally straightens up and puts his fingers on Sonny's chest and gives a little push. Sonny flies back about a yard. "You're an asshole," Wally says. "Look what you did to my door."

Wally bends over to have another look.

Sonny is moving his hands nervously, looking at Wally's back. I can see Sonny's face and I can see that he's scared. Still, he steps forward and grabs. Wally turns around, lazy looking and slow, and drops his right shoulder for the uppercut. Sonny reels back and hits the road with his ass. He sits there on the asphalt. Wally climbs back in. Steve titters. Wally walks back to his seat and sits down. "No damage," he says to me. Frank winks.

Nick backs up a bit and then guns the motor-home around Sonny's pickup. Sonny is sitting on the road with his legs splayed out in front of him, holding his gut. He looks ashamed, although he's done nothing to apologize for. Wally says, "Well, we bailed you out again, kid. We bailed you out so many times, I don't know...I suppose we're even going to have to figure out some way to bail you out with your wife."

Late that night, a little after we crossed the border, it's quiet and everybody's snoozing and the camper is rocking gently with the highway rhythm. Frank and Wally are talking quietly up in front. Frank is driving and Wally's lighting the cigarettes and talking, keeping Frank awake. I'm lying in my sleeping-bag on the floor in the aisle between the breakfast nook and the three-way fridge and every little crack and swell in the road comes up through the springs and chassis of the big motor-home and jiggles gently into my shoulder-blades. The lights of cars run in shadows across the roof and the miles flow by below. Out there in the dark, Ontario lake-country has already turned to Minnesota iron range and in another few hours we'll be down into the Wisconsin dairylands; every passing headlight and vibration from the road is bringing me closer to home, and trouble, and lies, and doors and windows and all the same bullshit as always. Funny thing is, I'm trying to keep that one memory intact, of that morning after I slept with Diana, how good it felt with the sunshine and the bare rocky island and the clean blue sky. So sad, when you know the truth. Finally Wally looked at me, with that tough-guy smile on his face. "Whatsa matter kid, feeling a little crabby tonight?"

I took the cigarette that Frank offered. "Very funny."

I sat there with my back against the three-way fridge, smoking. Wally and Frank were quiet for a while. Finally Frank looked at Wally. "Should we tell him?"

Wally looked at Frank. "I guess so...I guess we've initiated him enough."

Frank looked over his shoulder at me. "You can relax, kid. You don't have the clap."

I stared at them both, not understanding. "What do you mean."

"What the guide told you was all bullshit. We put him up to it. Didn't you see Steve laughing there at lunch-hour while the guide told you?"

"No."

Wally shook his head. "You're gullible, kid. You gotta work on that."

I thought about this for a few minutes. Then I leaned forward and pulled the keys out of the ignition. I forgot that the steering-wheel locks. Frank shouted and the motor-home lurched and we almost rolled over as he hauled it down and stopped dead at the edge of the ditch. Shouts inside, people waking up... I grabbed my bag and pushed my way out the door, threw the keys back at Frank with an overhand. "Take your job and shove it, Frank."

Wally looked at me like he was going to pop me in the mouth. "You little baby...you know what you almost did?"

70

I walked about 30 feet down the road, trembling, I was so angry. I didn't even know where we were. Farm country, somewhere. A yard light off in the distance, a dog barking. The motor-home started, muttering like a vacuum cleaner. Red fog drifted across the tail lights. I heard Frank's voice inside, addressing Wally, who was standing by the open door. "Go get him. Tell him we'll buy him a cheeseburger up the road."

Wally walked toward me. "I don't know what your problem is.... You nailed the biggest fish and the best-looking broad. It's us that should be mad at you."

I turned away in disgust. There was a faint green phosphorescence in the northern sky, up where Canada would be. I looked at Wally, the ex-soldier, who in silhouette looked like a chubby youngster, even down to the cowlick. "Don't be a sore loser," he said. "We give the new guy a hard time …it's a tradition."

There was no point in arguing with him about what they'd done to Sonny, or Diana. They didn't care. At the time, I hadn't cared either. It was a tradition. If I got back into that camper I was going to end up exactly like them.

"Come on," Wally repeated, a note of warning in his voice. "We don't have all night."

I hooked the bag over my shoulder, hesitating.

"Come on…no hard feelings. You're one of the boys, all right?"

I shouted over my shoulder as I was walking away. "Not yet I'm not."

The Survivalist

At dawn, in late April, after a long night of hard rain, a young Indian man named Sonny Copenace came steering his freighter canoe up the river. It had rained all night and was raining still, just a fine drizzle that stitched the air and muffled the noise of his passage, which was slow and uncertain, almost defeated by the rotting ice that clogged the slow-moving black water in the channel. On either side of the river steep rocky walls rose up, upholstered with tufts of blueberry and jack-pine. The rattle of the outboard seemed to answer itself in the narrow canyon. The rock walls rose up and the rain needled down.

The young man slowed the boat and grounded it on a mud flat where a little creek came into the river. He pulled a rusty old Lee Enfield .303 out of its vinyl case and said "Come on, Luke," to his dog, a sodden brown mutt that tugged on the leash with a squeaky whine as they crossed the mud flat and struck up into the woods. After hiking for several minutes through the dripping brush the young man yanked deftly at the dog's leash and paused, peering into the heavier spruce woods ahead. He stood for a long minute, frowning, biting his lower lip, as if debating the wisdom of proceeding any farther.

He was a guide and his guests, two German bear hunters, were supposed to be hiding in these woods somewhere. The trouble was, he'd left them out here all night long and he was uncertain about what he was going to find. Two rich tourists, dead from exposure? Two maniacs with magnum rifles, ready to beat the daylights out of him in revenge? He tried to image how he would feel if he were the one who had been abandoned in these dripping woods. He pondered his various excuses, trying to decide which one sounded most convincing. "I couldn't get my kicker going...I, uh, couldn't get the boat through the ice, awful ice jam, down there near the landing...."

The dog lifted his leg and delicately annointed a nearby stump, glancing up at Sonny as if expressing his own opinion about Sonny's immediate future. Sonny frowned again, and peered into the dark spruce bog ahead. He shifted the rifle off the shoulder sling and into his free hand, and moved forward. He tried to shrug off the uncomfortable sensation that he was being observed at this very moment through the crosshairs of a telescopic sight.

When he reached the clearing where he had last seen his guests he tiptoed forward. The bear bait—a sack full of hog mash and rotten meat—still hung untouched. He moved past the bait and a branch cracked like a gunshot right above him; he lifted his face and was driven to the ground as if by God's descending hammer. Breathless, flattened, he fought against the whirling crushing avalanche of boots and fists and sodden grunting masculinity. He clawed and bit and fought for his life, knowing in his quiet desperation that they had dropped from the tree right on top of him, and now they were going to kill him if he didn't get out from under their crushing weight. Finally he broke away and sprang to his feet, grabbing at the knife he wore on his belt. The cruel-looking one with the bald head rose slowly from all fours and edged toward him. "So sorry about that Sonny, so sorry..." he extended his hand and smiled fawningly. "So sorry...can we shake?"

I'm not falling for that old trick, Sonny thought. He let the bald one get one step closer then he swung his Kodiak up hard into the man's crotch, feeling the satisfying thump and seeing the big man fold up and go down like a sledged steer.

Sonny turned to the other, the red-headed man with the moustache, who was just now scrambling to his feet, and made a threatening move toward him as well. "How about you? You want the same?"

The chubby one with the red moustache held up his hands and shook his head rapidly. "Oh no, no...no Sonny, but thank you."

The bald one clambered to his feet, grinning fiercely through a face that was creased with pain. "Good deal, Sonny," he whispered hoarsely. "Thank you...thank you."

Diana rang up Sonny's drink on the till and came back to the bar stools and rejoined him. She propped one denim-clad hip on the bar stool and sipped languidly at her drink. It was Tuesday afternoon in the beer parlour and rain was drumming on the windows. "So then what happened," she said.

"Well...maybe they didn't really mean to attack me, I don't know. I saw all these cigarette butts on the ground under the tree, like they'd been up there all night.

74

Supposing…supposing they climbed up the tree during the night, because they were scared, then fell asleep on a branch up there, then woke up and fell right on top of me when I came to get them…?"

Diana giggled, then hid her mouth in her drink. The two hunters were sitting at the other end of the bar, and every time Sonny or Diana glanced in their direction they smiled broadly and gave a little wave. They were both wearing smallish Tyrolean fedoras.

Sonny knew that they didn't speak English but he nevertheless felt compelled to whisper. "Yesterday, I left the dog in the cab of the truck and he ate our lunch, cleaned out the whole damned box except for a bag of flour. So do you know what we were forced to have for lunch? Big gobs of bannock, mixed with swamp water and cooked on sticks over an open fire. Christ…I'm charging these guys for steak and serving them bannock…I'm leaving them out in the bush all night long, sitting in a tree, and they keep saying 'thank you, thank you…'"

Diana flipped her hair back and lit a cigarette. "Weird guys."

"Bear hunters, eh, what're you gonna do." Sonny shook his head and sipped at his drink. At the far end of the bar Burt Harrison and Willy were shooting pool. The click of the balls and Burt Harrison's loud voice combined with the rainy afternoon dirge of a David Bowie song on the jukebox. "Let me show you something…" Sonny whispered.

He reached into his pocket and pulled out a crumpled banknote. "You know what this is?"

Diana leaned against him and studied the bill. "A German dollar," she said.

"They call 'em Deutschmarks. You know how powerful these are?"

She shook her head.

"Guess," he said. There was a note of sorrow and resignation in his voice.

75

"I don't know."

Sonny nodded. "They're real powerful. You can buy a lot of stuff with one of these."

She lifted a skeptical eyebrow.

"These guys carry a roll of them this thick——" He held up his thumb and forefinger. "And you know what else?"

"What."

"These two guys belong to some big hunters' club in Germany. Strictly rich guys. If I show them a good time, they said they'd get all their buddies to 'start studying.' I guess they take this bear hunting pretty seriously."

Diana eyed the two bear hunters. She patted Sonny on the knee. "If you get more of those dollars we should go to Winnipeg."

Sonny nodded. He was in love with Diana and she teased him just enough to keep him hoping. He sipped his beer and thought about it. A weekend in Winnipeg with Diana would be like dying and going to heaven. But first he'd have to get these guys a bear. And with the way his luck had been going he'd probably find it easier to score himself a harp and a cloud.

In the woods the bear suddenly reared up on its hind legs ahead of them. At its feet was a broken log that seemed to be smoking: a rising cloud of wild bees. The dog gave a sharp yelp and bolted forward, hitting the end of the rope. Sonny had just pushed his way through the cedar boughs and because it was mid-afternoon and they were nowhere near a bait he was totally unprepared for the bear, just as the bear was totally unprepared for him. The dog hit the rope hard this time and the flimsy cord snapped in Sonny's hand. The dog was free and he charged across the clearing, his head low and his back legs pistoning furiously. Sonny swore loudly in Ojibway. As the two hunters blundered into him he threw up the .303 and flicked off the safety and squeezed off one round at the bear's face, knowing before he even jerked the trigger that he was going to miss by maybe a yard, and as the recoil slammed back into his shoulder the dog was on the bear and they were rolling over on the ground, a whirling clump of black and blond fur, and the two hunters were shouting excitedly and raising their guns and Sonny had to slap them and say, "No don't shoot, you'll hit my dog!"

The bear gained its feet and sprinted into the undergrowth, Luke the dog was so close to his rump it looked like they were attached. The cedar branches sprang back and forth, proving the bear had been no hallucination. Here was their one big chance and they'd blown it. "Come on!" Sonny shouted, pointing in the direction of the disappeared animals. "We have to run after them!"

The two men nodded rapidly. "Ja, ja…good deal."

Sonny had no idea if the two men were capable of running to catch a limber young black bear, but now that the dog was free there was no alternative. He couldn't leave the two hunters here, because they'd never find their way back to the road, and he couldn't leave the mutt to mix it up with the bear, who would soon enough begin to wonder why he was putting up with so much aggravation from an animal one third his size. Sonny slung his rifle and ran after the dog, and the moustached hunter ran after Sonny and the bald one brought up the rear. Sonny ducked under limbs and jumped over fallen trees, checking periodically over his shoulder to see if the two men, pink in the face and ponderously cantering, were managing to follow him. The trail led downhill through the rain-dripping woods, through a muskeg bog, thick spruce thickets that Sonny bulled his way through, and then back up a steep brow of granite where the bald-headed one slipped on the greasy moss and went down like a horse, grunting as his rump hit the rock. "Come on!" Sonny said, pulling at the man's arm. The dog's angry chopping bark was still within range but they weren't gaining any on the chase. "Come on!" He prodded the two of them up the hill.

Down a steeper ridge on the other side, slipping on the wet granite and sliding the last steep frightened second down into the waist-high sawgrass of a beaver slough. Through the slough, paralyzing black cold water and wet up to the crotch. Up the hill, down the hill, up the hill again. The two fat men coughing like outboard motors, their faces blue and berry-red and their eyes watering from the repeated whipping of branches. The dog sounded as if the bear was starting to circle, circling back as pursued animals do. The bear will just circle like this, all day if necessary, Sonny thought as he ran. These guys are never going to get a shot. Not only that, maybe one of them keels over with a heart attack any minute now... He could imagine driving back to the lodge with both guests lashed across the fenders, Bears 2, Hunters 0. And what was worse—no tip.

When they crossed the spot where they'd jumped the bear Sonny called a halt. You could barely hear the dog anymore and the two men looked like they were incapable of staggering another step. They were both in bad shape. The bald one had banged his head on a snag and there was a thin bloody line across the top of his head. He was making a sort of whistling sound when he breathed. The other one was half bent over, with his hands gripping his knees, and he looked like he was either going to pray to God or dump his breakfast. Sonny unhooked the plastic water bottle from his belt and took a mouthful of water, swilled it around and spat it out. He handed the canteen to the bald one, who was staring at him with a kind of strange, glittery look. "Don't swallow it," Sonny said, shaking his finger. "No swallow, no swallow."

The bald one seemed to think that Sonny was refusing him a drink of water. His jaw opened in a look of disbelief, then he turned away, nodding. "Ja, okay...good deal."

These guys don't understand a word I say, Sonny thought to himself. He walked over the the log where the bear had been digging at the beehive. Only one or two bees were flying in and out now, but you could hear the humming inside. He strolled across to the other side of the clearing and took a leak. You could barely hear the dog now, two miles away at least. Other than that, just the silence of the woods, a whisper of rain, wind in the treetops and the men muttering to each other in German. They seemed to be recovering, stripping off their pants and emptying the water out of their boots. They were ringing out their pants and laying everything on the beehive log to dry. On the beehive log to dry... On the—

Oh no, Sonny thought to himself. He turned around just in time to see the two men, in their baggy undershorts and knobby knees, batting the air and leaping up and down in an insane silent dance as the air around them filled with an angry swarm of wild bees.

"Dr. Rogers, Dr. Richard Rogers..."

"Dr. Bach, Dr. Helga Bach..."

Sonny sat in the waiting-room of the emergency ward at Kenora General Hospital, reading a *People* magazine. Every once in a while a nurse would go squeaking by and he would glance up expectantly. But still there was no word. The man in the chair opposite, also reading a magazine, had a large wooden fishing lure dangling like a decoration from the side of his head. He hadn't even been spoken to yet. Sonny was beginning to suspect that this was going to take all night.

Eventually a pretty young blond woman in starched whites stepped into the waiting-room and said, "Sonny Copenace?"

Sonny stood up. "That's me, nurse."

"It's doctor, if you don't mind...Dr. Bach," the woman said. She had a slight European inflection.

"Sorry."

"That's fine. Are you the tourist outfitter?"

"Well...I'm a hunting and fishing guide."

She nodded. "Your guests have been very badly stung,

79

I'm afraid. We're going to have to keep them for several days."

"Are they going to be all right?"

She nodded grudgingly. "They will recover, of course, but they're both quite badly injured, and obviously exhausted as well. Fortunately, I speak a little German and I've managed to reassure them, I hope."

Sonny exhaled. "Boy, that's good. I was kinda worried about them."

"Yes, they've mentioned your name too. They obviously admire you a great deal."

"They do?"

"They ask about you constantly. They keep insisting that you'll be angry if they miss classes tomorrow."

"Classes?"

"At the training school... Don't you run one of those Indian wood-lore schools for executives? Where they go and take endurance tests? That's how they explained it to me."

"No...I'm a guide. That's all."

She smiled. "Well...that's not what they think. You're a real slave-driver to them. These men run huge corporations at home and they sit in swivel chairs all day. They're not accustomed to being...pushed around, shall we say?"

"Right...no, yes," Sonny replied, half nodding and half shaking his head. "I guess so."

"I don't know what the appeal is, but they seem to love it. I suppose it can be boring always being the boss."

Sonny nodded, "Sure."

"There is only one thing that's been bothering them."

"What's that?"

"They want to know if they can come back next year. They're worried that you'll think they don't have the right stuff."

Sonny frowned. "Oh...they're worried... Well, I don't know what to say. They gotta get in better shape. One day they'll be out there and I won't be around to help them."

"I think they understand that."

"Tell them I'll think about it. Okay?"

The doctor smiled. "They'll be waiting on pins and needles for your decision."

Diana popped open the can of Miller and handed one to Sonny. She lay back on his fringed buckskin jacket and looked downhill toward the lake, where one of the new pupils was standing waist deep in the water, trying to catch a survival dinner with a stick and a string. The orange sun was sinking on a jagged horizon of distant spruce forest and the lake echoed with the hysterical giggle of a loon. The dog was snoozing in the grass beside them. "So this fat guy, Karl, wants me to come to a big sports show in Hamburg next year," Sonny said. "He says, take along some slides, Indian handicrafts, moose antlers, stuff like that. You could make some of that nik-nik tobacco and sell it in those little pouches your mother makes."

Diana lifted her nose. "Yuck. Nik-nik tobacco? They'd buy that?"

"Sure. And this guy, Karl, he says the whole trip is a business expense. Maybe could travel around a bit too. You ever been to Paris?" He knew she hadn't been to Paris.

She smiled at him through a dangle of shiny black hair. "Paris? What happened to Winnipeg?"

"Okay, maybe we'll spend a few days there too." Sonny sipped on his beer and studied the lake.

Back in the woods was the insistent hollow knocking of a hatchet on wood. Two of his other students were back in the forest, building a survival tree house. No frauleins allowed. In another few minutes he'd go and check on them, but right now it didn't sound like they were going to be finished before dark. The fourth man he'd sent down to the swamp to gather some cattail tubers for dinner, but it didn't seem he was having any better success. Oh well, Sonny thought to himself, they'll learn. And even if they don't, there's noth-

81

ing like a hungry stomach and a few thousand mosquitoes to build the old endurance.

"Another two days for this group?" Diana asked.

"Yep," said Sonny. "I'll leave them out here all night, and then first thing in the morning we'll go bear hunting."

"Bear hunting? I didn't see any guns."

"I make them use sharpened sticks. Guns are too easy."

The man who'd been fishing ran up to them excitedly. His pants were soaked and there was a small jackfish wiggling at the end of the string.

Sonny affected an angry look and wagged his finger. "No, no...nein!"

He muttered to Diana. "Look at the size of that thing... it's just a baby!"

He pointed to the lake. "Go on! Catch another one! That's too small...zu klein!"

The sportsman looked momentarily disappointed, then he managed a smile, a click of the heels and an obedient bow. "Ja, Sonny, good deal...thank you."

Sonny nodded tolerantly and lifted a finger. "Ja, ja... don't mention it."

The Window

In the last hour of the night Ed Taylor woke up and realized there was a prowler in the cottage. At first he wasn't sure what had disturbed his sleep; there was a mosquito marauding around his ear and he swatted at it and rolled over on the pillow. His wife was sleeping heavily at his side and there was a hint of daybreak in the window. Then he heard the footsteps, loud and obvious, in the living-room. He first thought, there's a bear in the house. The he saw the human shape sliding furtively through the living-room. A few moments later there were rustling sounds in the bush alongside the cottage, then a gradual return to quiet. A squirrel whirred somewhere out in the yard. The sky, after five minutes, was rapidly turning grey. Ed got out of bed and tiptoed across the floor into the living-room.

The screen-door in the kitchen was still hooked and un-opened, just as his wife always insisted on leaving it. The doors out to the verandah were heavy oak and glass and couldn't be opened from the outside. They were undisturbed and solid. The long windows along the verandah were all open or half-open. In one of the windows, second from the end, the screen was missing and Ed could see that it was lying outside on the deck. Ed put the window back in place and redid the latch hooks. His heart was still trotting. When he turned around he looked above the fireplace and saw the gun was missing from the wall.

When his wife woke up she found Ed searching through the living-room, opening drawers and spreading the contents on the living-room table.

"What are you doing up so early?" she said.

He smiled. "Oh, just tidying up."

"You're making a worse mess than there was."

She went into the kitchen and began making coffee.

Ed went down to the boathouse and had a look around. Every time he noticed something missing he made a note of it, and in several cases he could see that the prowler had looked at something then thrown it on the floor. He'd planned to tell his wife about it as soon as she walked into the living-room. He'd taken it for granted, in fact, that he would tell her.

But he hadn't told her, and now with the sun high and birds singing he felt he could no longer delay doing it.

Ten minutes later his wife called him for breakfast. They ate out on the sundeck, sitting at a small round table that overlooked the lake. It was an emerald-green August morning. His wife brought him slices of grapefruit and a platter of toast. He drank his coffee and feigned interest in *The*

Financial Post, trying to conceal the deep knot of anxiety that was still tight in his stomach.

After breakfast his wife came out wearing a yellow pant suit and carrying her purse. "I'm going shopping then I have a class this afternoon. Do you need anything in Keewuttunnee?"

He looked up from the newspaper and shook his head. "Nothing I can think of."

"I should be home around four.... There's a pork roast on the counter. Could you start it in the oven at about three o'clock, at 350?"

He nodded. "Sure."

He watched her walk down to the dock and untie the boat. The engine bubbled to life and she waved up at him, then slowly drove off. In several minutes she was only a spot out on the glittering blue lake, then the spot disappeared. Ed got up and went into the cottage to telephone the police.

An hour later the police boat pulled up to the dock. The constable climbed out; a moustachioed young man in tennis shoes and a baseball hat. They went up to the house and Ed showed him around. Several things were missing: an old banjo, a pork-pie hat, a framed photograph from the living-room wall. None of it seemed to make any sense. The .22 rifle was on a table out in the yard, right where Ed had found it. Ed had the presence of mind not to touch it, and he was carrying some pliers in his back pocket in case the constable had to pick it up. The constable picked it up, but he didn't bother with pliers. He pumped the action several times to make sure the rifle was empty then he handed it to Ed. "You want to wipe that dew off the barrel," he said.

They went into the house and the constable sat at the table and wrote down Ed's statement. When it was over he told Ed that stolen property was difficult to trace, especially when it was of no particular value. Also, he didn't know what kind of character they were dealing with here, somebody who would pass up the stereo equipment and a cabinet full of liquor in favour of an old party hat. Just as he was leaving he suggested that Ed have another look around the property, and maybe he'd find some of the other things too.

Ed spent the rest of the morning taking careful inventory of everything in the cottage. He wondered how he was going to break this to his wife. It bothered him that the policeman hadn't taken his complaint more seriously, and he'd given the impression that this case would be filed and forgotten. The old banjo, the photograph and the party hat might be worthless by some people's estimation but they dated back to Ed's youth, in college in Toronto, and they were worth more to him than any drawer full of jewellery. You couldn't write that on a police report though. You couldn't talk about how it feels to have your last refuge in the world broken into and ransacked while you're forced to lie there and listen.

By the time his wife came home he was so nervous that when she slammed the door his heart skipped a beat. She deduced that he was in some kind of mood and cooked dinner quietly, setting the table and sitting down across from him without once asking about his afternoon. After dinner he retreated to his stuffed chair and thumbed listlessly through a Pearl Buck, a novel he'd been trying to finish all summer. This summer there hadn't been any children or grandchildren coming to stay. There used to be a real clan, several years ago. Now one of the daughters was down in New Zealand, another in Edmonton. His youngest son was divorced and ran with a bunch of other 35-year-old adolescents. A week ago they'd been up here using the cottage and had left it a mess. Liquor bottles in the bedrooms and ruts in the lawn where they'd torn up the grass with one of those big motorhomes. Nobody cared about the family cottage anymore, that was clear. It was far too big for two people and the annual expense was shameful, when he thought about it. There was no good argument for not selling the place and if his health didn't bounce back he probably would.

Ed gave up the book and went to bed. He put on his pyjamas and turned off the lamp and closed the door, climbed into the bed and pulled the quilts over his head, turning away from the crack of light that poured in from under the door. Somewhere in the other room was the sound of Barbara Frum and the *Journal*. In the bedroom the smell of the forest drifted in through the screens. Ed travelled into sleep, leaving it all behind. He was going into a dream and he was flying slowly, slowly, because he was entering this dream reborn as an albatross. He was a wandering albatross, the largest kind, with a great angel-like pair of wings that spread over ten feet. He was a special albatross, one that had lived for over a thousand years, and he was gliding only a wingbeat above the surging ocean. He flew for an hour like this, not caring about whatever direction he flew in, then he landed on a huge green wave and rested. He settled his head under his wing and slept for a while, and the wave rocked him back and forth. In the albatross dream he began sinking deep down into the ocean, into the deeps of cold and darkness, and then there was a terrifying pressure on his chest and a sinister creak of approaching footsteps and he came awake with a spastic jolt, certain that now somebody was coming into the room.

His wife was sleeping in bed beside him. The windows were open, and from the cold air in the room he knew it was late. He lay unmoving and strained his ears in the silence, and listened to the trees creaking outside in the wind. He lay like this for an interminable length of time, and when the sky began to turn grey with the light of dawn he finally fell back to sleep.

When he woke up it was 10.30 in the morning and the sun was in the yard. He could hear his wife operating the weed-eater out by the flower garden. He got up quickly and dressed and went out into the kitchen, barefoot. His wife had set him a place at the table and the newspaper was folded

87

beside it. He peeled an orange and poured a cup of coffee and carried the tray out onto the sundeck. He was coming through the double doors when he saw the old photograph in its neat wooden black frame sitting on the window-ledge.

He sat down, stunned, on the top step. The prowler had come back! His imagination had not been playing tricks on him. Last night, when he woke up, the thief had probably been standing right at the bedroom door.

He went into the cottage and made a cursory search, and discovered that two more articles were missing: an old leather bomber jacket of his from the war, a bottle of $20-scotch from the liquor cabinet. This became obvious after only a quick search around the house. What might turn up missing after six months or a year was anybody's guess. What he couldn't figure out was why the framed photograph had been returned.

He went out into the yard and walked around, searching the ground for clues. The lawn was dry and woolly and snagged with crisp yellow leaves. There were some tracks of cloven hooves along the edge of the garden. At one point he looked up and saw his wife watching him. She was on the aluminum ladder with just her head showing above the roof, watching him the way you'd keep your eye on a child. He knew what he must look like, poking around in the leaves with his pyjama top on, at quarter to twelve in the morning.

His wife was going to go to a ceramics class at the canoe club this afternoon. This was the final day of the course, and then came the Labour Day weekend, and then back to the city. If it weren't for her class this afternoon he might have suggested that they pack up and head for the city right now, but then the cottage would be unprotected and he could spend a lot of time feeling guilty about having left it that way.

The place was built by his father in 1915, and Ed practised the upkeep of it like a small religion. The lawn was not good; acidic soil, and not much of it, so that their front yard was just a thin scalp of green stretched over smooth granite. But the bedrock made for solid buildings. The cottage was as square and firm as the summer it was built, and with its high domed roof, and outstretched verandah wings it looked like some huge shingle-feathered bird nesting among the trees.

Ed skipped lunch and went straight to work on the windows. His wife wanted to know how he was feeling and he told her he'd had indigestion through the night; that's why he'd slept in. His wife was finally developing an affection for the cottage after all these years. When the kids were young it was just one chore after another, laundry by hand, cooking, guests dropping in, not to mention the mice in the cupboards, the bugs, and soupy August drinking water, crawling with life. Now, just as she was beginning to relax and enjoy the place, he'd have to tell her, not so fast dear, there's a robber under the bed.

As soon as she'd gone off to her class Ed went into the cottage and telephone the police. There would be no half-hearted responses this time. He wanted results. Constable Chaput, the same one as yesterday, answered the phone and Ed informed him that the prowler had returned. The constable didn't seem overly disturbed at this news and he replied that if Ed would tell him what additional objects were missing he'd add them to the list. Ed replied without hesitation that he'd supply no information until the police reported to his residence in person, and without all the usual shoulder-shrugging and delay. The constable replied coolly that this would not be possible today, but that he would take the details over the telephone, if Ed wanted to furnish them. Ed felt like shouting into the receiver, but after seething for a moment or two he told the young constable he wanted to speak to his superior officer. This didn't seem to ruffle the man either, and he assured Ed that his sergeant would be quite willing to talk to him, but he wasn't in the office today and Ed would have to call back tomorrow. So Ed

89

hung up the telephone and went out into the backyard, thinking that the local cops really were jerks, just like his son had always told him.

He worked all afternoon, until he could feel the sun burning on the top of his head. He pulled the shutters out of the storage shed and leaned them alongside the cottage. He washed them down with the hose and after they were dry he touched up the worn spots with a small brush and a tin of green paint. The shutters were notched with Roman numerals and Ed cleaned out the lines with his pocket knife, then moved down the rear wall of the cottage, lifting each shutter into place and nailing it in. Soon the entire back wall and most of the side of the cottage were closed in and impregnable by any means other than violent break and enter. The windows on the other side and front wing of the cottage were too high off the ground to worry about, unless the burglar happened to bring a stepladder. After he was finished he stepped back and spent several minutes standing there with his arms clasped across his chest, studying his handiwork.

Next he went into the toolshed and searched through the bottles and boxes of spare parts until he located a sliding dead-bolt for the back door. The dead-bolt was still wrapped in its original brown paper bag, purchased before the days of bubble-form plastic packaging, and the price was still crayoned on the paper: 45 ¢. In another bottle he found three old .22 cartridges, which he dropped in his pocket. He took down a chisel and a square and a Philips screwdriver and went out into the sun.

An hour later the back door was done; a bolt that snicked smoothly into place, and looked strong enough to resist a pair of Pittsburgh Steelers linemen. Ed went around to the front door and studied the old hasp and lock, but it had been mounted properly many years ago and it looked as strong as the day it was installed. He put the tools away and took an old empty motor-oil can off the shelf and went out into the yard and set it down on a stump beside the toolshed. He went into the cottage and got the little .22 pump gun off the wall and went out and sat on the back steps. The motor-oil can was about 40 feet away. Ed took the cartridges out of his pocket and cleaned them off. The brass was tarnished and the lead was greasy and covered with lint, which he cleaned off with his thumbnail. He fed them into the tube and pumped once. The oil can was an easy oblong of red and silver in the sights. He squeezed the trigger and nothing happened.

It's no surprise, he thought to himself. The gun was almost an antique, a 1910 Winchester with the blueing rubbed off the barrel and a stock that was battered and worn. Ed lowered it from his shoulder and held it in both hands and read the inscription on the barrel. The gun spat like a cat and the bullet ticked a tree somewhere across the yard.

Ed shook his head and sat looking at the gun for several minutes, holding it carefully now, as if it might be even more dangerous if he put it down. He pumped out the empty shell and once again took aim at the oil can, resting his elbow on one knee. The bright red of the label steadied around the front sight and he squeezed the trigger. There was no response but he held his aim and waited. The seconds counted four and five and then there was a crisp snap and one of the toolshed's little windows blew out.

Ed pumped out the third cartridge and put it in his pocket. He went to the toolshed and put the gun up amongst the rafters, and then swept the broken glass off the floor. Enough of this nonsense, he thought to himself. He was glad the gun didn't work. He went out into the yard and stood around for several minutes, trying to think of something to do until his wife came home. It was the hottest part of the day and his head and neck were beginning to ache. He pulled the handkerchief out of his back pocket and wiped the greasy film of moisture from his forehead, then climbed the stairs and sat down in a wooden chair on the deck. There would be a few moments when he'd forget about the burglar, and then the thought would come back again. He'd been thinking that if he got some sleep now, just a nap, he'd be able to stay up much later tonight, keep the lights burning; and he could read. It probably wasn't a bad idea to rest for a while, in any case.

He tipped his head back in the wooden lounge and stared out at the lake. The water was slack and smooth in the afternoon heat. Overhead there were fronds of spruce and through an opening in the branches there was a curve of egg-blue sky. He was thinking about being down in the hospital centre's basement several weeks before. It was a labyrinthine, dismal underground complex, with long winding hallways that smelled of formaldehyde and little rooms with heavy concrete walls. He remembered the little windows in those rooms, how you could see out through the bars in the windows to the trees and the sky. They'd brought him to this room to do a brain scan, which meant putting radioactive liquid into his veins, and then taking pictures of him with some huge and ominous-looking camera. The doctors had clustered like sub-hunters around the radar screen, and its green glow illuminated the room. Occasionally one of the doctors would say that he'd spotted something, and his finger would touch the glowing screen and the others would squint and look closer, hesitant and unsure. Meanwhile he was laid out in a kind of dentist's chair, with a plastic oxygen hose in his mouth. All around him and over him were the mazes of lights and wires and hoses, and he felt like he was floating up toward that little window, with the bars on it, and the square opening of sky.

His wife came home at five in the afternoon and she told Ed she was glad he'd installed the shutters—now the awful job of closing was half done. Tomorrow morning they could start packing, and by noon they'd be ready to go. Ed nodded, unwilling to get involved in their annual argument on the subject. Leaving a day early meant missing the heavy

Labour Day traffic. But it also meant missing a full day at the lake. Normally Ed argued in favour of staying, but this was not a very restful vacation, and the doctors had warned him to be well-rested when he checked into the hospital on Tuesday. His wife was probably thinking the same thing, but she knew better than to remind him of it.

They went to bed after the *National,* and Ed read for a while after his wife went to sleep. Ed turned out the light and lay awake for a long time, listening to the intermittent gusts of wind through the trees, and far off the rumbling door-bang of thunder. He stayed awake, hoping that the thunderstorm would come their way, but after a long while the sound of the storm faded. The wind was still active in the trees, and he fell asleep thinking how unusual it was to have a warm summer wind on this late weekend of the year.

Dawn. He was awake. His heart was banging. Outside the bedroom window he could hear the slow stealthy crush of footfalls in the dry leaves. The sounds were coming closer and he could hear the faint click of contact now, on the shingles of the outside wall. Ed struggled as if pinned on the bed, and uttered a fearful grunt. The sound of his own voice seemed to snap the restraints that paralyzed him and he came off the bed in a rolling sit-up, his bare feet hitting the floor. The screen seemed to bulge inward, with a spruce branch against it that was shaped like a hand. Ed fumbled on the night-table and seized a ball-peen hammer and stood in a half crouch, his rear end against the bed, his hammer arm cocked, facing the window.

He waited.

Minutes went by.

It began raining, or always had been. The rain would scuttle on the roof in big drops and then nothing, just the swish of the wind. He strained his ears, and shivered as lightning flicked outside. He moved to the bedroom door and peered into the living-room, where each shadow looked like a murderer frozen in mid-step. Finally, after minutes of

93

watching and waiting he realized that the living-room was empty. He tiptoed into the kitchen and checked all the doors—locked. He checked the front door and found that it was bolted and tight.

He walked to the window and stood there, looking out into the yard. With the rumble of a stone being raised from a pit the thunder began rolling, and though it was raining only fitfully the yard was lit on and off by the steady pulsing light. There was nothing and no-one in the yard, and Ed could see that even the oil can was still sitting on the stump, blindfolded, waiting to be shot.

He went into the kitchen and sat down, and a few minutes later his wife came out and put her hand on his shoulder. He put his arm around her waist. "The thunder woke me up," he said.

She scratched a wooden match and lit a candle.

"I thought I heard somebody at the window," he said.

She nodded. She went to the stove and touched it and a blue crown of fire rose on the ring. She began mixing something into a pot on the stove. She poured in two cups of milk and set the pot on the flame. "We'll have something to drink," she said quietly.

They sat at the table and the storm echoed all around, and the rain came to the roof with the sound of soft hammering. The clock on the wall said six o'clock, but the blackness showed no sign of the coming dawn. When the hot chocolate was ready they went into the living-room and Ed lit a small fire of broken lumber and pine knots. They sat on the sofa in front of the fire and drank hot chocolate, and sat quietly waiting for daylight, when it would be time to start thinking about going home.

Talent Night

Late in the day Chaput pulled into the driveway of the police station and parked, climbed out of the car and put on his hat. The Sergeant hadn't yet left for the day—his Cordoba was parked beside the black-and-white police Suburban. Chaput walked up the flower-trimmed sidewalk to the front door of the red brick OPP station. It was a cool and gloomy September evening. There were yellow poplar leaves all over the green lawn and the petunias were dying. Winter is coming, Chaput thought to himself. At the boot scraper beside the front step there was a pair of overturned rubber gumboots. The boots were black rubber, with rolled-over cuffs. Chaput saw the word LOVE inscribed in red lettering on one boot and the word HATE written on the other. Chaput pulled open the door and went inside.

"I'm late," he announced.

Murphy was sitting at a typewriter, jabbing away with two fingers. He glanced at Chaput but didn't say anything. The office was full of the smell of Borkum Riff pipe tobacco, which indicated that Sergeant McCandless was behind that half-opened office door, probably discussing some crucial paperclip allotment with his colleagues in Kenora. Chaput hung his hat on the hook. The boots of prisoners were kept outside so that they wouldn't smell up the office. "Who's in the jug?" Chaput said.

Murphy didn't answer. His face was impassive and his eyes were focused on the report he was typing. Chaput opened the steel door and went into the room containing the jail cells. There were three cells, small enamel-painted rooms about the size of a large broom closet. Each cell was equipped with a rubber mattress thrown hippy-style on the floor and a bare toilet bolted to the wall. There were no windows. The bars along the front still smelled of a recent coat of government-issue green enamel. In the third cell, sleeping peacefully on the mattress, was Sonny Copenace. He was lying on his side and his hands were folded between his knees. He was wearing a fringed buckskin jacket spread across his shoulders like a blanket. His ponytail was knotted with red yarn and there was mud all over his jeans. Chaput was mildly surprised to see Sonny in the cell. At this jail they had lots of repeat customers from the Indian community but Sonny wasn't one of them.

Chaput walked out into the office and closed the steel door behind him. Murphy was dabbing white-out on the triplicate report. In the other office Chaput could hear McCandless talking on the phone. Something about getting a price on a home-video unit. Free long-distance telephone courtesy of the province, Chaput thought. Must be nice. "What's he in for?"

Murphy rolled the report back into the typewriter. He gave a desultory flick of the head, a gesture that Chaput assumed was intended to pass for an answer. Chaput slid into the swivel chair on the other side of the desk from Murphy and deliberately kicked the typewriter's plug out of the wall with his toe. Murphy's eyes lifted slowly. Chaput wore a bland expression.

"You unplugged me," Murphy said.

"Oh sorry. Did you want me to plug it back in?"

Murphy gave Chaput his best Legs Diamond I-oughta-kill-you stare. Chaput sometimes felt like taking Murphy outside and washing his face with mud. "If you would just open your eyes," Murphy said delicately, "and look behind you, you would see the reason Mr. Copenace has been arrested. Now would you please plug in my typewriter?"

Chaput turned around and saw a banjo leaning in the corner. On the chair beside it was a pork-pie hat. Chaput stood up and checked out the banjo. Murphy, in a silent fury, got out of his chair and jabbed the plug back into the wall. Chaput strummed a few notes on the banjo. It was a mile out of tune. The pork-pie hat was too small. "Where'd you get this stuff?" he asked. Murphy one-finger typed, ignoring him. Chaput frailed the banjo, seeing if he could remember "Oh Susannah." He was a little rusty, complicated by the fact that he'd never really learned how to play the banjo in the first place. McCandless appeared in the doorway.

"You're the first guy to come in here today that can get a sound out of that thing," McCandless said. He had a pencil and a piece of paper in his hand.

Chaput sat down in the swivel chair and settled the banjo on his knee. "I always wanted to get one of these but my mother made me take the clarinet."

McCandless nodded, thoughtfully puffing on his pipe.

He was a handsome individual, sandy-haired with a cavalryman's moustache. With his tweed jacket, broad shoulders and steely blue eyes he would have passed for heavy police intelligence of some kind, the chief of papal security perhaps. The pipe, which he puffed on incessantly, gave him an aura of calculation and cool intellect. Anyone who spent any time with McCandless soon realized, though, that his brain was set permanently in neutral. He was the perfect living proof that upward mobility in the OPP hierarchy was basically a beauty contest, determined by cleft of chin and grace of gait and utter lack of intelligence, or so Chaput had decided. McCandless released great plumes of perfumey smoke as he stood beside Chaput, watching. "By God it makes you want to break out the old harmonica, doesn't it?" McCandless remarked, glancing at Murphy. Murphy kept typing. "I don't listen to no music unless it's Elvis," he said.

His repertoire exhausted, Chaput lowered the banjo and studied the name that was engraved on the neck. "Ed... Taylor... Jeez, that name is familiar. Where have I heard that name?"

"Don't strain your brain," said Murphy. "You were only at his cottage three days ago."

Chaput reexamined the banjo. "Hey...this is the one he reported stolen."

"Brilliant."

Chaput looked at McCandless, who was turning the pork-pie hat in his hands as if it were the most fascinating thing he'd ever seen. "One of the cottage people called me on the weekend on a B & E," Chaput said. "Gave me a list of stuff a mile long, and kept calling me back and adding stuff. You know...giving me the latest update. He told me his .22 had been stolen and I found it on a picnic table in the yard. A bit forgetful, this old guy. Anyway, I thought he imagined the whole thing. But what do you know, here's his banjo." Chaput looked at Murphy. "He was really hot over losing this banjo. You're quite a hero, John. Was it Sonny had it?"

Murphy nodded. "Claims he found it in the woods behind the guy's cottage."

Chaput said, "Maybe he's telling the truth...why would he just swipe a party hat and a banjo?"

McCandless raised an eyebrow. "That's a valuable instrument."

"I suppose...you know, I wouldn't mind swiping one myself."

Murphy elaborated. "I went into Yelle's house this morning and saw Sonny sleeping on the couch with the pork-pie hat on. He had his arms wrapped around that banjo. I saw the name plate on it and remembered that old guy with the burglary last weekend."

McCandless piped a huge column of smoke. "Good work Murphy. Damned good work."

Murphy grumbled. "And you know what? In another day or two it probably would have been used for firewood."

McCandless looked at Chaput. "And as for you...when you've finished making fun of your partner raise this Taylor fellow on the telephone and tell him we've located his merchandise. I'm sure he'll be appreciative."

Chaput leaned the banjo in the corner. He flipped open his notebook and looked up Ed Taylor's number. He picked up the phone and dialed the number. He listened to the phone ringing. Along the bottom of Chaput's telephone were four buttons. Three of them were clear plastic. The fourth was a red one beside which he'd pasted a label that read PANIC BUTTON. There was no answer. He hung up. "No answer," he loudly announced.

McCandless and Murphy were talking about the VCR units that the local store was selling at deep discount. Their heads swivelled simultaneously and they looked at Chaput. "Then drive out there and see if he's home," McCandless said. "If you leave it he's going to close up his cottage and be gone and I'll be tripping over that damned banjo for the rest of the year."

Chaput shrugged. Fine with me, gentlemen. Your company isn't exactly fascinating anyway. He slapped his hat on his head and took the banjo and tucked the funny hat under his arm and took the keys for 302 down off the hook and went outside. Dusk. Windy and cold on the lawn. He walked down to the patrol car and put the banjo in the back seat and got in and started the car. He drove down past the train station and the community hall and Steve's Esso and out onto the pale dusty washboarded gravel road leading out of town. Bang rattle bang. He drove fast on the rippled road with the dust unravelling in the rear view. Four minutes out of town he made the left turn onto the bush road leading to Cottage Blk. 3. The road was a humpy, winding path through the woods, toothed with stony ridges that could tear the belly out of a car if it was driven much faster than a walk. When he got to Taylor's cottage the windows were boarded up and there was no sign of anyone. He checked the back door, which was padlocked, and went around the front. A boat was overturned on the lawn with a tarp over it. There was an oil can sitting on a stump by the woodshed. Chaput got back in the car and U-turned on the lawn. It was getting dark. It had blown rain all day but now the sky was clear and sundown was a big smear of colour through the broken trees. Chaput sometimes felt a twinge of depression coming out here. The woods had a tricky way of repeatedly reminding him what a complete non-event his life was. When he got back to the office Murphy was gone and McCandless was all trenchcoated and ready to hit the trail. Their day's work was over and Chaput's was just getting started. "The place looks closed for the season," Chaput said, leaning the banjo in the corner. "I'll check around and see if I can dig up the guy's city address."

McCandless lit and re-lit his pipe, peering out the window as if checking for the Clanton gang, then lifted a hand to Chaput and said that he guessed he'd pop home for some chow. McCandless invariably referred to food as "chow" and sleep as "shut-eye." Chaput waved benevolently from the corner of the office where he puttered with the kettle. "See you tomorrow."

Chaput finished making the coffee then lit a cigarette and sprawled in the swivel chair. The guard sheet was on the desk in front of him. At the top of the guard sheet was the prisoner's name, Sonny Copenace, and the time of booking, 11.20 AM. The entries stretched almost all the way down to the bottom of the sheet, marked off in twenty-minute intervals. Beside each notation either Murphy or McCandless had scrawled an OK and their own initial, indicating that Sonny was still alive and snoring. Murphy had a habit of working all day and then filling out all his OKs in one fell swoop but McCandless was a stickler for regular checks and Chaput was new enough here that he still tended to do things by the book. After finishing his smoke he went in and checked on Sonny, who seemed to be having a pleasant restful evening if no-one else was. He went out and marked OK on the sheet. He leaned back in the chair and stretched the long muscles in his arms, cracked his knuckles. It was a long swing until 2 AM. He sipped at his coffee and smoked another cigarette. He went in and checked on Sonny, marked an OK on the list. Interesting to calculate how much money is spent annually so that dangerous banjo thieves can get lots of supervised rest. He browsed through a hunting-magazine that Murphy had left on the desk. "Bucks to Brag About," "This Happened To Me." Chaput wasn't big on blood sports. His life was already quite adequately furnished with scenes of carnage, thanks. His last flirtation with the sportin' life involved an attempt to pot a ruffed grouse with his service revolver, a point of aim slightly lower than it should have been splattered a technicolour mess of eviscerated grouse all over the road. A beautiful wild thing instantly transformed into dogfood, theoretically to save the $1.75 he would have spent on a Teenburger and bring him close to nature. He put the magazine away and looked out the black window, wondering if maybe the phone would ring. He needed a little crime to alleviate the boredom. He got up and went to the corner and picked up the banjo, sat on the edge of the desk. He tried a few chords, lightly tapping the sharp strings. I had a dog and his name was Blue. I had a dog and his name was... I had a dog and? Chaput thought that you chorded a banjo just like a guitar with two strings missing, but he couldn't remember which two strings you left out. He heard a rattling cough in the other room and a metallic clank. He laid the banjo on the desk and opened the door leading into the cells.

Sonny was leaning against the bars. "Hey Chaput... Gimme a drink."

Chaput went into the utility-room and rinsed a plastic milk pitcher under the faucet. He let the water run for a minute then filled the pitcher half full. He went back to the cell and gave it to Sonny. The haggard-faced young man drank the water for a long time. He lowered the plastic container and handed it back to Chaput. "You got a smoke?"

Chaput lit a cigarette and handed it to Sonny. Sonny nodded and turned away. Chaput went out into the office and closed the big green door behind him. He sat down in the swivel chair and propped the banjo on his knee. He played for a minute or two and then Sonny's voice came through from the cells. "D chord... That's a D chord for that song. Christ, you sound like you're walking on it. It's D and then special A."

Chaput tried the chords Sonny suggested. It still didn't sound right. He was assuming that he and Sonny had the same tune in mind.

"Special A, special A..." Sonny chided. His voice had the disengaged tone of someone sitting on the toilet.

"What's 'special A?'" Chaput inquired unenthusiastically. "I've never heard of it."

"That's where you hold your two fingers together only with the string in between."

Chaput sat there, trying to decipher the instruction. He tried several combinations then stood up and went into the room with the cells. Sonny's tattooed forearms extended through the bars. His forehead was resting on the bars and his long fingers held the smoking cigarette. Chaput stood there and strummed a chord. "This one?"

Sonny shook his head. He reached through the bars and re-positioned Chaput's fingers.

"That's an A seventh," Chaput said. "Not a 'special A.'"

Sonny gave an unconcerned shrug. He blew a tired plume of smoke. Chaput experimented with the two chords. He could switch from one to the other, but it took him three or four beats to realign his fingers. He tried it for several minutes then rested, his fingers stinging. He examined the tips of his fingers then tried playing it again. He looked at Sonny. "Then what."

"G chord."

"How do you make a G chord with four strings?"

Sonny tapped on the frets. "Here and here."

Chaput handed him the banjo. "You do it."

With the cigarette dangling from the corner of his mouth Sonny took the banjo and held it as best he could through the steel bars. He plucked it and adjusted several of the tuning pegs, then played a rollicking melody with his fingers dancing up and down the neck. Chaput stood with his arms folded, watching. Sonny played for maybe 45 seconds then stopped and demonstrated the chord transition, blowing smoke from his nose.

Chaput took the banjo and tried it again. Terrible. He was getting worse instead of better. "I can never remember where you switch to the tonic chord."

"The what?"

"The tonic chord."

Sonny shook his head. "It doesn't matter about that. Just

play it."

"What do you mean, 'just play it.' I don't know *how* to play it, that's what I'm telling you."

Sonny thought about this for a moment. He smoked the cigarette and looked at the banjo. Finally he took the banjo from Chaput and started to play the tune, slowly. "Don't watch the fingers," he said. "Listen to the music."

He and Chaput locked eyes, nodding to the exaggerated rhythm of the melody. "Tell me when to change," Sonny said.

Chaput frowned, nodding. "Now!" he said. "Now." He listened to several bars, calling out the chord changes.

Sonny nodded. He handed the banjo back to Chaput. Chaput played the chord progression again, listened to the music and tried not to think about it. He could feel a sudden impulse to change chords. Sometimes he was right and sometimes he wasn't. He was more accustomed to playing music according to rules. He shook his left hand and gave the banjo back to Sonny. "Ouch."

Sonny held the banjo, running his hand up and down its neck as if patting a dog. Chaput went into the utility-room and got one of the steel folding chairs, set it up in the narrow space in front of Sonny's cell. He sat down and lit a cigarette and crossed his legs. "Go ahead."

Sonny played the banjo without even looking at it. The cigarette hung from his mouth and his eyes looked away through the bars out toward the office and the dark September night beyond. His fingers danced and scuttled on the strings, making a sound so wild and free that Chaput felt chills running down his back.

After playing for several minutes Sonny paused and threw the cigarette into the toilet. Chaput was wooden-faced. He folded his hands over his knee. "Do you think you could teach me how to do that?"

Sonny did a 30-day bit in the DJ in Kenora and got back to

Keewuttunnee in early October. Sharp frosty mornings now and the annual passion play of dying leaves. Early in the mornings the sun would break over the eastern hills like a molten weld; instantaneously the town would flood with light. Chaput was motoring across the tracks one morning when he spotted Sonny coming up the right-of-way. He rolled down the window and waited. "You're back from holidays."

Sonny shrugged. Jail was no big deal to him either.

"I bought something in Kenora last week." Chaput pulled the car off the tracks and got out. He opened the trunk and pulled out a hardshell banjo case. He flicked open the latch and displayed his new toy. Disgraceful waste of money but what else were you supposed to do in this dead-end town. Chaput handed the banjo to Sonny.

Sonny examined it, his face expressionless. He ran his hand down the neck, smooth wood. He nodded and gave it back to Chaput. "Nice."

"So are you going to give me lessons?"

Sonny shrugged.

"How about tomorrow night," Chaput said.

Sonny nodded.

"I'll meet you at the daycare at seven," Chaput said, climbing back into the patrol car. Chaput got McCandless' wife to give him the keys to the daycare centre and he went over there at seven the next night. He thought it was a good neutral place to meet. He went in and turned on the lights and uncased his banjo and his clarinet. He hadn't played the clarinet since high school but he still had it kicking around. At twenty after seven Sonny still hadn't shown up so Chaput got in the car and drove over to the reserve. He parked at Yelle's house, where Sonny often stayed, and walked up the mud sidewalk to the front door. Two dogs followed him, growling. A little girl with big un-Indian blue eyes opened the door. Sonny and five or six other guys were sitting in the front room watching the hockey game. They looked at

Chaput, no doubt wondering why he was here in denims and a lumberjacket instead of the usual military garb. Without saying anything Sonny got up and grabbed his jacket and joined Chaput at the door. The little girl stood watching with wide eyes. Her mother was Diana Highway and Sonny was supposed to be the father. Diana was off partying in Kenora, the last Chaput had heard. Sonny patted the little girl on the head. "I'll be back tonight."

Sonny followed Chaput outside. They drove over to the daycare centre. Chaput made coffee while Sonny sat in the corner looking at the banjo. Sonny had a sour expression on his face. Either he didn't like new instruments or he'd rather be home watching the hockey game. The ceiling of the day-care centre was forested with cardboard elephants and zebras and bunny rabbits, which hung so low that Chaput had to duck and weave his way through them with the coffee in his hands. They sat at a table by the window in little chairs with their knees in front of them. Chaput was beginning to wonder if this evening was such a good idea. Sonny looked embarrassed to be stuck in here with some klutzy, off-duty cop and anyone driving by could see them sitting in here in their kiddie chairs. However, they'd come this far so they might as well take a stab at it. Chaput opened his banjo case and took out a packet of John Denver and Gordon Lightfoot songbooks and suggested that Sonny flip through them and find one that they could try. He said for now Sonny why don't you play the banjo and I'll play the clarinet. Sonny settled the banjo on his knee and Chaput cleaned the clarinet's reed with his fingernail. He blew an experimental squawk. He was in the high school band the last time he played this thing. Sonny started plunk-plunking the banjo and Chaput played a wavering first note. Three hours later they were still jamming.

The next Tuesday they met for another practice, same time same place. Chaput wasn't getting much chance to play his banjo but he was re-learning the clarinet, and enjoying it. Sonny would lay down the rhythm with the banjo while Chaput tooted out a sad quavering melody line to "Amazing Grace" or "Early Morning Rain" and then they would switch; Chaput would blow backup while Sonny climbed the neck of the banjo. By the end of the evening there was a gang of little faces at the darkened window, and all evening cars had been slowing down to peek at what was going on in the daycare. The next morning it was snowing. McCandless called Chaput into the office and notified him that he'd received a complaint from the Chief and Band Council on the reserve. Chaput rolled his eyes and sighed. Now what.

"They say that the daycare centre is a government-funded operation and should be available to everybody in the evenings, not just the cops."

Chaput shrugged. "So I don't care if they come and use it. I'm not stopping them."

The next Tuesday night it was cold and blowing snow. When Chaput arrived at the daycare centre with the key there were already two sullen-looking Indian youths waiting at the door. They had long hair and wore high-heeled boots and they looked almost frozen. The one in the brown vinyl jacket was carrying an uncased and battered old guitar. Chaput made coffee and he and Sonny went about their business, trying to ignore the guitar-plunking competition on the other side of the room. This pair, whose names were Stan and Henry, favoured the modern top-40 for material. Stan would strum the guitar while Henry crinkled his eyebrows in pained sincerity and mewed some Hall & Oates composition. Chief Romeo Star, an overfed and self-important bureaucrat if ever there was one, showed up in the latter stage of the evening and idled his four-wheel-drive outside on the parking-lot, shining his headlights in the window to ensure that everything was proceeding fairly. Then just in case he hadn't been noticed he came and wallowed in the foyer for five minutes, observing the proceedings with a hurt and suspicious expression. The next Tuesday night when Chaput arrived Chief Romeo Star had opened the daycare centre with his own special key and he was already in there, showing off to Stan and Henry with his big blue electric guitar. Musically speaking Chief Star was lodged somewhere back in the nineteen-thirties, back in the early fusion years of the Appalachian murder ballad and the cowboy she-done-me-wrong song. He would wail a Carter Family or Jimmie Rodgers song in such a passion of nasal mispronunciation that Chaput would pause at the banjo and look up and then double-look just to make sure that the man wasn't experiencing a brain seizure. Three musical acts at cross-purposes in the same room were bad enough but the following week old Charlie New York showed up with his fiddle along with a white social worker from the reserve who suffered from a weird misapprehension that he could play the flute. Halfway through the evening McCandless and Murphy showed up, looming big and ominous in the foyer in their dark OPP winter coats, and the music took a distinct nosedive as they stomped the snow off their boots and came in. Stan tuned his old guitar and grinned nervously, no doubt thinking in terms of outstanding warrants, of which he and probably half the young Indian men in Keewuttunnee had plenty. McCandless, pleasant dumbbell that he was, didn't seem to notice the damper that his presence had put on things. He fired up his pipe and loitered by the finger paintings, listening to the welling chorus of squawks and twangs and tweets and nodding approvingly as if it were a Mozart opera. Strolling over to the piano he stood with his hands folded behind his back and watched the social worker from the reserve stumble through "Stardust." Chaput took five for a smoke break and went outside and stood in the softly falling diamond snow. The police car was sitting with its motor running on the road in front of the daycare. When Chaput went back inside Murphy was standing by the piano with his coat off crooning out some half-comic Elvis Presley impersonation while Romeo Star strummed along and everyone else clapped and laughed. What a showoff, Chaput thought.

Christmas in Keewuttunnee was a bit of a non-event. A lot of people had hometowns elsewhere and disappeared for a few weeks. The handful of townspeople with reasonably profitable occupations usually made a big deal about going off to Hawaii or Roratonga or someplace. The town settled into a deep winter silence, enshrouded in ice fog. Usually somebody froze or burned to death just to provide a counterpoint to the season. Rita McCandless, the sergeant's wife, was involved in the town festival committee. Every Christmas she and a group that everyone referred to as the Bible-Bangers sponsored a supper at the town hall. All the town kids would run around whooping like Indians, which they were, while their parents sat solemnly waiting for John Murphy's Santa to arrive. Two weeks before Christmas she approached Chaput and suggested that it would be wonderful, so very wonderful, if they had a sort of Keewuttunnee Talent Night this year, featuring some of the "talented boys" who played regularly at the daycare centre. Chaput announced her suggestion at the next Tuesday night meeting, although he wasn't too fired up on the concept. Nobody here could really play worth a damn except for him and Sonny, and getting up on stage with the rest of them would only make him look bad by association. The others weren't very enthusiastic either. "Why doesn't she get some funding from Indian Affairs?" said Romeo Star. "That woman, she always wants us to do things for free."

Chaput went to Rita McCandless and told her that there would have to be an incentive of some kind, if not an outright payment maybe a prize. Something appropriate. He suggested that she go to the music store in Kenora; maybe there was a gift certificate or a used guitar or something. Chaput didn't feel entirely comfortable talking to Rita about this. The winner wasn't supposed to pick out his own prize.

Within a few days Rita had organized the whole thing. Posters all over town announced that a TALENT NIGHT! would be held on a Saturday evening, 21 December at the Keewuttunnee Community Centre. Rannick's Music Emporium in Kenora had given Rita a big discount on a MYSTERY PRIZE! that was enclosed in a big red velvet Santa Claus-type sack, and was now being displayed, along with an advertisement for the talent show, in the front window of the Bay store. The following Tuesday night Rita came by the daycare centre and talked to all the musicians about rules of procedure. It was agreed that each act would be limited to three songs or ten minutes, whichever came first. Sequence would be decided by drawing lots just before show time. The winning act would be chosen by the audience, who would indicate their approval with applause. Chaput cast his eye over the motley gathering. You certainly had to hand it to these people—willing to get up in front of everybody and make fools of themselves. Even Murphy seemed serious about entering. He was sitting on a school desk in the corner with a solemn expression on his face. Chaput tried to imagine Murphy crooning out some insipid Elvis Presley song, and hoped that when the time came he wouldn't burst out laughing.

The big night was only ten days away and Chaput used every opportunity to meet with Sonny and practise their act. The daycare centre wasn't always available, so they'd meet either at Chaput's trailer or Yelle's house, practising in the kitchen while kids ran around and the living-room hockey fans roared. If nothing else, he was learning a little about everyday life on the reservation. One night, while they were playing in the kitchen, he overheard somebody in the living-room talking about a stolen car and he looked at Sonny with an expression of mock horror. Oh my goodness.

He was working the night shift later on in the week and he smuggled his clarinet into the office and kept it in his evidence drawer. Late at night when the town was quiet and the owls were hooting in the woods a quavering melody would drift out of the yellow-lit windows of the OPP station. Just around the corner in Pig Hollow where the police residential trailers were located a scratchy old recording of Elvis Presley's "Love Me Tender" rolled out of the lit windows of John Murphy's double-wide. Across the frozen bay on the Indian reserve, the sound of a slurred passionate hillbilly ballad echoed inside Chief Romeo Star's house. From other houses came the thumping of guitars and the feline yowl of violins.

Two days before the contest Murphy and Chaput were in Kenora for a court appearance. Afterwards they went for lunch at the Husky. Murphy had been acting very strangely lately, almost like a normal human being. Chaput couldn't fathom it. Not only did Murphy compliment Chaput and Sonny on their musical talent, but he also paid for lunch and offered Chaput his second-last cigarette. Heading back home it occurred to Chaput why Murphy was in such a good mood. Murphy was telling him a funny story. It concerned a conversation he'd had with Chief Romeo Star. Murphy asked Romeo to play backup guitar for him on "Heartbreak Hotel." Romeo had agreed to do it but with some reluctance. "As long as everybody doesn't expect me to play for them," Romeo had said. Murphy laughed, looking at Chaput. Isn't that funny? Didn't Chaput think that was funny? Here you try to lend a guy a little credibility, give him a shot at the brass ring, and he acts like he's doing you a big favour or something. Aw, to hell with him. Murphy didn't want to share the prize with the slob anyway.

Chaput just sat there, looking out at the unwinding backdrop of snow and rock and forest. Did Murphy actually think he was going to win? And Romeo Star, too? It would be comical if it weren't so annoying. It seemed like the only way you could get any respect in this town was to never say what was on your mind, just keep on bullshiting and acting like you'll never lose.

The Keewuttunnee Community Centre was a corrugated
metal building with a hockey rink outside. Even with
Christmas lights strung on its wooden falsefront it still
looked like a big sewer pipe. Inside, there was a plywood
floor with chairs and tables stacked along the wall. At one
end, a wooden stage. At the other the kitchen and bar and
washrooms. The contestants began arriving long before the
audience. A few late entrants signed up. Sam Morrison
(dressed like Bob Dylan, carrying a six-string guitar) and
Johnny Newcombe (whose notorious poverty had earned
him the nickname Johnny No-Cash) drifted in and were
assigned numbers by Rita McCandless. Chief Romeo Star,
at the last minute, had pulled out of the competition,
explaining to Rita that he wanted to "give some of the
younger fellahs a chance." Offering to act as an emcee
instead, he proposed to introduce each act and maybe play a
song or two in between. All the different groups milled
around backstage, nervously reciting cue cards with lyrics
printed on them, tuning their instruments and glaring at
each other. On a table in front of the stage the Mystery Prize
sat in its red cloth sack.

At eight o'clock it was show time. Only about a dozen
adults and half as many children sat in the hundred-odd steel
chairs that had been set up in front of the stage. Rita con-
ferred with Romeo and made the decision to hold off for
fifteen minutes. Sam Morrison, in his nerd-style Bob Dylan
sunglasses, sniffed in amusement and lit a cigarette. "It's
Christmas time, 30 below. I figure everybody's probably at
home slashin' their wrists."

At fifteen minutes after eight there were about twenty
people in the audience, not counting the pack of little kids
who were tearing around playing keep-away with
somebody's wool hat. Romeo Star whispered to Rita
McCandless, high-signed to Chaput, and then plugged

in his guitar and pranced out onto the stage. "Hellooo...
Keewuttunnee!" he exclaimed, bowing and waving to the
audience. He immediately hit a chord on his guitar and
launched into a spirited rendition of "Hey Good Lookin',"
completely screwing up the lyrics in the second verse and
faking his way through by smiling radiantly and repeatedly
chanting the phrase "How's about cookin' something up for
me." When the song was finished he grinned and bowed
from the waist and raised his hands in protest. "Thank you,
thank you...you're a beautiful audience."

Chaput peered around the edge of the stage. They were?
The first six rows of chairs were mostly empty, except for
McCandless, who was sitting near the front off to one side.
The audience, for what it was worth, was generally made up
of the old women of the reserve, who usually attended every
event in Keewuttunnee no matter how boring. With their
modestly folded hands and tightly bunned hair and suspicious expressions they looked exactly like a jury at a murder
trial. Children, hyperactive as squirrels, crawled all over the
long skirts of the old women and chased each other around
the rear of the room. It seemed that only two people
approved of Romeo Star's song, McCandless and Romeo's
mother. Both were hesitantly clapping.

"Our first act is a pair of fine, talented fellahs..." Romeo
Star announced. "All the way from the Keewuttunnee Indian
Reserve... Let's hear it for...Stan and Henry! Hey all right!"

Stan and Henry trotted on and did three very passable
tunes. Once again, there was little if any applause from the
audience. Chaput was beginning to get nervous. In theory,
it was nothing to go out there on stage. After all, this was a
hometown audience. But the butterflies in his stomach
fluttered wildly every time he thought of actually going out
there and smiling into the spotlight and starting his song.
Sam Morrison was next. He strolled out onto the stage and
stuck a lit cigarette between the tuning pegs of his guitar.

He played a rippling arpeggio with his fingernails and adjusted his sunglasses. He looked down at McCandless and inquired, rhetorically. "And where have you been, my blue-eyed son?"

Sam stayed on stage for a little over ten minutes, delivering a single long rambling Bob Dylan ballad that kept on going when everybody thought it was over. Romeo Star got up and destroyed another Hank Williams tune. Johnny Newcombe was next. The first song on his agenda was "Folsom Prison Blues." He got the first laugh of the night by putting on a gravelly voice and saying, "Hello...I'm short of cash." A few more adults had arrived, the Baptist minister and his wife—both of them prim clappers, the Harrison boys in their orange snowmobile suits and floppy boots and a group of surly adolescents who lined up along the bar in the rear. Now it was John Murphy's turn. Murphy had Brylcreemed his hair into a jelly roll curl and was wearing an Elvis-style outfit, a gangsterish black shirt and white silk tie, a big round silver belt buckle on his tubby paunch and pointy leather shoes. He had a towel slung around his neck and his collar was turned up. Murphy didn't have to look very hard to find an Elvis outfit because that was what he usually wore anyway. Romeo Star had finally consented to play instrumental backup for Murphy. Romeo hit the big B Seventh at the beginning of "Heartbreak Hotel" while Murphy, with the microphone in one hand, shot a finger at McCandless and musically informed him, in an angry baritone, that since his baby had left him he'd found a new place to dwell. By the time Murphy had hip-wiggled his way through the first verse and was gutturally grunting, "Ah feela so lonely baby," Romeo Star was helplessly lost, playing B chords instead of A and vice versa. The curled lip of Murphy's Elvis faltered. His half-closed eyes widened as he quickly glanced at Romeo Star to see what was happening. Romeo just smiled confidently, nodding his head and slapping the guitar rhythmically. Murphy briefly regained his equilibrium and then mixed up his lyrics and mysteriously found himself in the middle of "Blue Suede Shoes." Romeo wore his benign smile and tapped his toe while he strummed, pursing the side of his mouth and hissing at Murphy "Go straight into 'Hey Good Lookin'.'"

Murphy cancelled his third song and came backstage looking like he'd just run ten miles. Chaput and Sonny were next. Chaput's fingers were shaking. Sonny had a butt hanging from the side of his mouth and didn't look the least bit nervous, but that just made Chaput feel worse. Chaput looked at Rita. "Maybe we should call an intermission." Chaput looked around at the others but they didn't seem to have heard him. This is it, he thought. We're going out. "Okay Sonny, are you ready?" The Harrison brothers were booing and Romeo Star was trying to placate the crowd.

A crumpled paper cup floated down out of the darkness and bounced at Romeo Star's feet.

Sonny glanced offhandedly at Chaput. "I don't really think we should go out there."

Chaput answered quickly. "You're right. We're too lousy. I'm too lousy. Somebody good should be next." He looked at Charlie New York. "What about you Charlie... couldn't you be next?" All of the Harrison boys were booing now.

Charlie shrugged. He looked at Chaput. "I'll go out if you come with me."

Burt Harrison foghorned from the back of the hall. "We want a refund!"

Chaput looked at Sonny.

Sonny nodded. "I'll go out if Charlie goes out."

Stan and Henry walked up. "We'll come out too. It's better with everybody."

Murphy overheard the plan. "Listen...I got shafted. If you guys are taking another shot at it, then I'm coming out too. What song do you want to do?"

There were two or three minutes of discussion and dissent

and then there was a long silence backstage. Romeo Star walked out into the spotlight and said, "Thank you, ladies and gentlemen, you've been a great audience. And now... for our last act of the evening...just before we ask you to select a winner...I'd like to present a special last minute entry...The Daycare Singers!"

Romeo clapped wildly while everybody trooped onstage. Then he evasively slipped around and joined them. Fiddle, harmonica, clarinet, guitars, banjo and vocalists all positioned themselves with frantic whispering. Romeo, on rhythm guitar, looked at everybody and said, "Okay you guys, on four, okay?"

As soon as Charlie New York started to play his violin, that sweet haunting opening line of "Amazing Grace," Chaput knew that they weren't fooling around anymore; this was the real thing. Romeo Star thumped a gentle rhythm line on his electric guitar and the other instruments tiptoed in one by one. Murphy leaned into the microphone and began to sing; the card with the lyrics was in his hand but surprisingly he seemed to know the words. Sam Morrison joined in, singing high harmony... *How sweet the sound / That cured a wretch like me / I once was lost but now I'm found / Was blind, but now I see...*

Sonny came in and did the next verse solo on the banjo, playing the melody slightly behind the beat, so that each note fell precisely into the expectation and the need for it, and straining forward, watching Sonny's impassive face and listening to every nuance of his fingerpicking Chaput had the strange sensation that he knew something now, about Sonny, that he'd never known before. He lifted his clarinet and began to play, communicating with Murphy and Stan Highway with nods and glances, and Stan answered by playing a pretty flamenco bridge up the neck of his steel string guitar. There were so many instruments and band members that by the time they finished the last verse there was time only for an everybody-sing chorus and a wrap and their ten minutes were up. Judging from the clapping in the audience and the rowdy cheering from the back of the room there wouldn't have been much objection to an encore but Chaput knew that it would probably be smart to quit while they were ahead. Everybody seemed to agree with him. They all bowed and trooped offstage.

Rita went out and did the applause judging with the audience. The audience clapped more for the solo acts now that they did before but there was no doubt, from the sound of the applause, that the impromptu band, the Daycare Singers, was the winning entry. The Mystery Prize was unsacked. Harmonicas and kazoos and penny whistles clattered all over the table. The band members handed them out to the kids, who took off and ran around the back of the hall tooting on the whistles like a pack of demented satyrs.

So the Talent Night turned out to be a success after all, at least in the sense that they all turned out to be contest winners. In the following months there were several Tuesday night meetings at the daycare centre but by March the attendance had fallen right off. Finally it was just Chaput and Sonny playing their instruments inside. And then Chaput had a touch of the flu one Tuesday night and didn't make it. Then for the next meeting it was Sonny who didn't show up. Chaput didn't feel all that disappointed. They'd both been getting a bit bored with it but neither one had wanted to be the one to call it quits. March turned to April and spring came to Keewuttunnee. Now it was melting snow and mild air and late evening sunlight when Chaput drove out to make his first rounds of the night. Pretty soon it would be summer, and this town would become the best instead of the worst place in the world to be. Outside of town there was a creek where the kids went fishing. Chaput pulled over and rolled down the window and watched for a while. Sonny was there, balancing on a stone with a long skinny poplar pole that had a wire noose at the end. He would pass the pole like a wand over the water, then he would dip the noose down into the sky-bright current and the pole would bend horribly and then out of the water would catapult a fish. After a few minutes Sonny stepped off the rock and picked up his heavy burlap sack and climbed up the bank. The bag looked like it had a child's body inside. He laid the pole down and took out his pack of smokes. He gave one to Chaput.

"Catching lots?" Chaput said.

Sonny gave the sack a little nudge with the toe of his rubber boot. The sack kicked back at him in return. "Lots of redhorse suckers. Good bear bait."

They watched in silence for a while, while the kids along the creek bank snagged and pestered the fish. Finally Sonny picked up his pole. "Well...I better go get some more."

Chaput nodded. "Yep..."

Sonny hoisted the sack onto his shoulder. "We should get together and play sometime, eh?"

Chaput nodded. "We should do that real soon." He eased the car into gear and moved away. He knew that they never would.

The Apprentice

The dragonfly nymph rose like a bubble of rotten froth to the surface of the water-filled ditch. Its stalked eyes broke through the surface and revolved like twin periscopes, taking in the sunbright world of the early June morning, the blue haze of sky above, the glossy green jungle of cattail and sawgrass leaning alongside the ditch, and the tiny beadlike tidbits that clung to the greenery and crawled on busy legs up and down the stalks...food. It unhinged its oversize jaws and edged its body around until it faced the direction from which its potential meal would likely come blundering. Its jaws hung open like a miniature trashcan and it faced the sluggish current in a condition of immobility, gradually blending with the surrounding vegetation until it seemed to disappear.

In the air above the ditch a one-day-old Damsel spider leaped from a branch and floated gently, lightly, obliquely down along a strand of silk that it had loosed several minutes before. The one end of the strand was fastened to a willow bud. The other end was fastened to a long slender metal rod with a tiny ball at the tip. The spider re-anchored the silk and spun another strand, back and forth, from the willow twig to the metal rod until the diadem angles of the web began to emerge. When the web was finished the spider moved to the centre of the pattern and melted into immobility. The sun bounced on the shiny lines of the web. The sun glinted on the silver car aerial the web was attached to, and on the chrome strip that ran down the edge of the police car fender.

The police car was parked in a thicket alongside a gravel highway. In the same thicket, in fact so close it partially obscured the parked car, was a large plywood sign facing the roadway:

KEEWUTTUNNEE INDIAN RESERVE
Band 49 Welcomes You
You Are Now Entering Ojibway Nation
NO LIQUOR Beyond This Point

Despite the stark black-and-white paint job of the police car, stencilled with serial numbers, and its twin red roof lights it was not a conspicuous feature of the landscape. The drooping foliage and the dark shade cast by the sign almost eliminated it from view. Likewise, the man leaning against the car was almost obscured by shadow. He was a strong, beefy-looking man wearing striped pants and a blue shirt and a belt over his shoulder. His elbows were propped up on the roof of the car and his eyes were pressed against a set of binoculars. As he adjusted the fine-tuning of the glasses the large muscles of his arms bulged unnecessarily. He lowered the glasses and wiped the moisture from his eyes. A single lock of blue-black hair dangled from his forehead. There was a scar on the bridge of his nose that he'd picked up the year before playing inter-tribal hockey. He lifted the glasses and focused on a plume of dust that was beginning to rise from the gravel road in the distance.

In the approaching car—actually a truck, a silver-grey Dodge Ram with factory air and tinted windows—was off-duty OPP constable John Murphy, tooling along home after a Monday shopping trip in Kenora, with his bags of groceries stacked on the broad bench seat beside him, the celery tops and green grapes and T-bones and booze all enclosed in air-conditioned comfort while the dust raged outside, and while Ricky Skaggs wailed about how he got his heart broke Murphy peeled the top from another tin of Molson's Golden and contemplated his upcoming evening: half a kilo of red meat and an unlimited beer source and the sublime pleasure of watching the Hamilton Tiger Cats hit the field for the first time this season.

Just as the reserve sign came into view Murphy smiled and spoke out loud. "Now ain't that cute," he said. He slowed the truck and rolled down the window.

The Indian man in the police uniform was walking out onto the road.

Murphy pulled up and stopped the truck. "Chopper... what the hell are you doing out here all by yourself."

The Indian man looked off down the road, as if avoiding the question. He looked back at Murphy. "Not too much traffic today."

Murphy was trying to keep a straight face.

Chopper referred to his notes. He was always recording things. "Three cars only..." he said. "A tan sedan, owned by the principal, and a blue pickup...no booze in either one."

"What about the other one?"

Chopper shrugged. "He just drove by. He wouldn't stop."

"He wouldn't stop?"

"That's right. Three guys." Chopper motioned with his hand. "They just...they just kept cruisin' right through."

Murphy nodded. It was getting to the point where this whole program was vastly amusing to him. Chopper was the fourth native constable assigned to him for training in two years, and not one had lasted six months on the job. Once they discovered there was more involved than cruising around in a starched uniform and pulling down 25 grand a year they started to get second thoughts. Chopper, although a brawny-looking type, was actually a mite delicate in temperament. Before signing up for the program he'd worked as a janitor in the school, pushing a mop and bucket around. That's where he should have stayed, Murphy thought.

Murphy sipped at his beer. "Buck up, Chopper. I'm back on the job tomorrow. We'll put you to work washing the police car or something."

Chopper nodded trimly. He made a note in his pad.

Murphy eyed the six-coloured ballpoint pen in Chopper's hand, also the new watch on his wrist, one of those pocket-calculator / stop-watch / beeper models. He shook his head and put the truck in gear. "I'll see you later. Don't hurt yourself."

"Everywhere we go we have to take Chopper," grumbled Murphy. "It's like always having your baby brother tag along."

Murphy had driven the car into the woods behind the boundary sign and he was already parked and out of the car and onto the gravel of the road, cleaning his Ray-Bans and scowling at the approaching vehicle. Alain Chaput, his partner, slammed the door of the cruiser and came out of the bush and Chopper, whom they'd literally left in the dust, came driving up in the BAND POLICE Suburban, with the wire-screen partition across the back and the red war eagle on the door and he parked it on the shoulder, no room for two vehicles in the access road, and climbed out and hurried up to join them.

Murphy raised a hand. "Stop. Stop right there. Where's your hat? How many times have I told you not to leave the cruiser without putting the hat on? And will you close the door of your truck for the love a Mike?"

Chopper spun on his heel and went back to close the truck door, which had swung open. Al Chaput slapped him on the back as he returned, hatted. Chaput still called him Noel, although Murphy's nicknames were usually too appropriate to resist. In this case he'd dubbed Noel Jonnie "Chopper" after the cartoon bulldog he closely resembled. Despite the hulking appearance and the broken nose and the underslung jaw Chopper, however, had the tender instincts of a mother hen. He would think nothing of spending ten minutes helping some worthless drunk up off the pavement, that sort of thing. Murphy probably had more the physical characteristics in mind.

"Now..." Murphy continued, raising a finger as if he were training a dog. "Go call headquarters and give 'em our twenty. And don't mumble, you should hear yourself on the radio sometime. You sound like Marlon Brando with a tennis ball stuffed in his mouth."

Chopper went back to the truck and made the call and they waited. A crow rowed across the sky above, its wings creaking.

After a minute Chopper closed the truck door and came walking back. "I made the call," he said.

"Good for you. Did you get any on ya?"

"Pardon?"

Murphy folded his arms across his chest. "Now Chopper, let's run through it all again. Today we're conducting searches. Do you remember the film we showed you on

123

searches?"

Chopper nodded.

"Okay...tell me how you conduct a legal search."

"Well, the, uh, legality of a search is, uh, determined by—"

"Wait, now. First things first. For the sake of an example let's say they actually obey you and stop. What do you do next?"

"Uh...I say, uh...good afternoon sir, we're conducting a liquor check and—"

"It's morning now, Chopper. It's morning."

He nodded nervously. "Okay, I uh, sir...we're doing a liquor check and—"

"Did you say good morning?"

"Uh, good morning sir..."

Al Chaput interrupted. "Here comes a car."

Murphy issued another hand signal. "Okay man, you're on." He turned to Chaput and shook his head, smiling.

A blue Toyota station wagon slowed, approaching. It had a woman driver. Chopper held up his hand and tentatively flagged her to a halt. "Uh, good morning miss," he said. "It's like, uh, we're checking for liquor, eh? And, uh..."

He paused. The exact wording...what was it? He'd memorized so many cautions and subsections and codes that with people staring at him he couldn't remember one from the other. Liquor, liquor... He looked off down the road, avoiding eye contact. "And, uh...I want to know if you're carrying any liquor today?"

The driver of the car was a white woman, one of the new government employees on the reserve. She thumped her palm against the wheel. "Actually I do have a bottle of wine. It's just for dinner. I'm not bootlegging or anything."

She pulled the wine bottle half out of the grocery bag, showing him.

"I'll have to take it, please."

She gave him the wine and he handed it to Murphy.

124

Chopper clicked the button on his ballpoint. "I'm sorry to give you a summons, but—" he shrugged, "it's the bylaw on this reserve that no liquor is allowed. Do you see our sign there?"

He flipped open the ticket book and Murphy slapped him on the back. "Good work, Chopper. I'll take over now."

Murphy handed the wine bottle back to the woman. "We'll just give you a warning this time, Frances. Chopper here is doing some on-the-job training."

She hesitated. "Oh...all right."

She put the wine bottle back into the grocery bag.

Murphy touched the bill of his hat. "Off you go, now. Don't worry about the wine. We don't usually bother with the teachers and that, as long as they have the liquor for their own private use and don't flash it around."

"Okay."

She shifted the car into gear and drove away. "Here comes another car," announced Murphy. "And these are Indians. Get out of the way, Chopper."

A lime-green station wagon with a bad muffler was rumbling slowly toward them. Inside the car were two people, a native man and woman. The man had a dark bony face and looked about 50 years old. He rolled down the window and stopped the car. He smiled broadly. His wife was not smiling. "Well by Jesus, John Murphy, you come and meet me again, eh?" the man chuckled. "We're getting to be good friends, you and me."

"Shut the hell up and step out of the car," said Murphy. "Chopper...go tell the woman to get out of the car."

"Noel Jonnie," said the man in the car. "You can't be a police. You're an Indian!"

Chopper went around to the passenger side and tried to get the woman out of the car. He opened the passenger door and the woman started yelling at him in Ojibway, wagging her finger furiously. Chopper took a step backward and hesitated. He looked at Murphy. "She's putting a curse on me."

Murphy yelled at the woman. "You! Shut up and get out of the car!"

"By Jesus, Murphy's mad today," said the Indian man.

"And you shut up too! Stand over by the police car!"

The man turned to walk toward the police car but Murphy seized his elbow. "First you show me where you hid that damn whisky. I don't have all morning to be tearing that damn car of yours apart."

"Whisky? What whisky?" The man looked at Chopper and gave him a sly wink. "That's a white guy's uniform, Noel Jonnie."

"You know what whisky I'm talking about. Now where is it? Is it in here?" Murphy opened the tail-gate of the car and rummaged through the piles of groceries, laundry, fish nets, tools. A wooden crate filled with engine parts caught his eye. "Aha! The old hide-the-booze-in-the-antifreeze-container trick eh?"

He hauled the antifreeze container out of the crate, popped the cap off and triumphantly emptied the contents on the gravel shoulder.

"Hey, come-on, Murphy... Jesus, dat's six bucks!"

Murphy fired the empty container into the ditch. "So you don't use that trick anymore, eh. How about these groceries here?" Murphy manhandled a box of groceries onto the tail-gate. "What have you got in here, syrup? Ha! I bet."

Murphy poured the syrup onto the gravel with the antifreeze. The Indian man just shook his head, silent.

"Well, what do you know? What have we got here?" Murphy remarked, daintily hoisting a bottle of whisky between thumb and forefinger. "It sure looks like booze to me. Chopper...write him up, possession of liquor on an Indian reserve. Here Al, evidence." Murphy tossed Chaput the bottle of whisky.

"Chopper, write him up," Murphy repeated. "Chopper ...?"

Chopper was getting into his truck. The engine roared to

126

life and the tires spat gravel as he accelerated away. Chaput watched the truck going away. Murphy was scribbling in his ticket book. "Where's Chopper going?" Chaput said.

Murphy's big shoulders lifted in a shrug. "I don't know," he said. He punched the button on the ballpoint and stuffed it back in his pocket. "Nor do I care."

Chaput planted a cowboy boot on the steel step of the jail trailer.

Murphy fired up the cigarette and carried on with his story. "So here I am, stuck with the new broad, this dickless Tracy, and naturally the first night we're out the shit hits the fan. We're driving along this dirt road on the east end of the reserve and this guy comes stumbling out of the darkness, waving his arms, covered in blood from head to foot, and he tells us that Rudolf Cocopenace is beating the shit out of everybody—he's gone berserk."

Chaput grunted in appreciation. Murphy tapped his cigarette. They were sitting on the front steps of the jail trailer, Murphy in uniform, Chaput in denim. This was a regular ritual, sitting out on the steps in the evening. The mosquitoes droned around their heads. In the west, above the ridges of granite and spruce, the sky was lit with the standard holocaust of colour as the day's light faded. "Now ...the last thing I want to hear in the whole world is that Rudolf Cocopenace has gone berserk, especially when I'm riding with a copy who wears perfume and weighs 106 pounds."

"Rudy Cocopenace...isn't he the one who looks sorta like Frankenstein?"

Murphy nodded. "That's him. So I follow this complainant back to his house, and his house is totally destroyed, smashed to smithereens, furniture, windows, blood, glass, people wailing and sobbing, pointing to the next house and saying, 'The bad one did it! The bad one did it! He's over next door!'"

127

"So I look at Debbie but does she look worried? No, of course not—she's wapping the old night-stick in her palm and saying, 'Well partner, let's go get him!' She's all keen like we're going to play tennis. It's only a hundred yards to the next house but we drive over, because there's no way I'm going into the dark after Rudolf Cocopenace without twin Dobermans and a chrome-plated shotgun. We get to the next house and it's the same thing, the door is kicked open, the furniture's thrown all over the front steps and the lawn, and the people are all covered with blood and they're screaming, 'It was the bad one! It was the bad one! He's gone thata-way.'"

Murphy twiddled the cigarette between thumb and forefinger. A mosquito settled on his neck and he crushed it with a wipe of his hand. "So round about now I think, maybe we'll skip a house this time. I kill the headlights and hustle on up to Joe Jack's house. We park the car and we're climbing the front steps when the door bursts open and Rudy Cocopenace runs out and steps on my head. You know, he comes running out and stomps on my head like a big cigarette butt. This puts me out of action for a second or two and Debbie, sweet little Debbie, throws her night-stick at him as he's running away and she gets lucky and tags him right in the shins and brings him down like a ton of bricks."

"Hey..." Chaput quietly cheered.

"So next scene...he's lying there on the ground and crying and shaking, crying like a 250-pound baby and I even get one of the cuffs on his wrist before he starts to cheer up. I'm sitting on top of him, I've got one cuff on one wrist, I'm holding his other wrist with both hands and suddenly he's not crying anymore, he's starting to laugh, then growl like a bear, and I've got his wrist in both hands but Jesus Christ *I can't hold him!*"

Chaput whistled.

"My two arms can't match one of his! So now he's gaining an inch, now two inches and in seconds he's going to free that arm and I'm in serious trouble. I'm not kidding, I'm talking serious trouble. I'm talking wheelchair, neck brace, full pension, the works." Murphy blew a thin stream of smoke. "So now I can't hold him anymore. I've had it. I'm about ready to drop his wrist and take my chances...curl into a ball and start screaming for my mommy when I hear him say 'Oh!' and I feel his muscles relax a bit. That's all I need. In a split second I got that other wrist handcuffed and that was the end of that...thanks to little Debbie."

Murphy took one last pull of the cigarette. He flicked it away and it fell in a long tumbling arc. The driveway was paved with Murphy's discarded filters. "That was ten years ago, more or less. And you know what? Little Debbie taught me something that night. She taught me that you don't have to be a big guy or a white guy or even a guy to do this job... you just have to know where the balls are located."

Chopper slowed the big Suburban and stopped at the boundary. He backed into his U turn rear end first, as Murphy had taught him, but instead of completing the turn he switched off the ignition and climbed out. Along the front bumper there was enough space for a car to pass if it drove partially through the ditch. Otherwise the road was effectively blocked. Chopper went down into the ditch and tested the ground with his boots, ascertaining that the mud was hard enough to drive on. A few weeks ago, he thought to himself, he'd have been walking in water up to his knees. Now the frogs were gone and the ducks have moved to the big lake. The air above him switched back and forth with dragonflies, a sign of mid-summer. He climbed out of the ditch and wiped the lenses of his sunglasses, trying to ignore the prickly dampness under his arms and the nervous chugging of his own heart.

In the dim reflection of the window he adjusted his cap and made sure his tie was knotted properly. He was a little surprised at how official he looked. The Sam Browne belt was looped snugly over one muscular shoulder. The bill of the cap rode low and businesslike and the expensive sunglasses made him look like one of those tough southern sheriffs. He turned around and saw a puff of dust rising in the distance and right away his stomach began writhing again.

The first car approached and he recognized the blue Toyota and the woman behind the wheel. He held up his hand in a signal for her to halt, feeling nicely seconded by the two-ton black-and-white behind him, and as she rolled down the window he spotted the top of the wine bottle protruding from the grocery bag on the seat beside her. "Good afternoon," he said. "We're running another check today. Are you carrying any liquor at all?"

Murphy thought maybe it was a smash-up or a construction crew blocking the road but when he saw the red roof lights up ahead he cursed and shifted the truck into four-wheel drive and drove on the shoulder. There were maybe a dozen cars lined up on the hot dusty gravel road and the drivers eyeballed him quizzically as he bounced past, no doubt thinking he was nervy to pass them like this with the cops ahead. The first car in line had its trunk open, Chopper was lifting out two twelves of beer and the principal of the elementary school was standing by, with a peeved expression on his face. Murphy parked his truck and climbed out, leaving it running. Somebody in the third car in line whistled at him; he was wearing Bermuda shorts. He gave them the thumbs up and approached Chopper.

"Chopper," he said evenly, "do you mind me asking what you're doing?"

Chopper's expression was unreadable behind the billed cap and dark glasses. After a moment or two he said, "I'm writing up a summons for Mr. Rebchuk, to appear before the magistrate on Friday afternoon, 11 August."

Chopper signed his name and tore off the sheet and handed it to the principal.

"Gimme that," Murphy said.

The principal handed Murphy the summons and he scanned it...no mistakes. He shook his head and handed it back to the principal. "You think I got all day to sit here in a line of cars?" Murphy said. "Move your truck. And next time don't block the whole damned road. I don't know what you're trying to prove with all this."

Chopper looked over at the ditch, where Murphy's truck was idling with its front bumper almost touching the bumper of the police truck. He looked at the cab of Murphy's truck, where a tin of Molson's was propped in the drink holder. Up and down the long line of cars people were standing outside their vehicles or sitting on their fenders, watching. Chopper noticed the lime-green station wagon and the man who'd had his syrup poured on the road by Murphy. "Okay..." Chopper said. "You're in a hurry?"

Murphy grunted. "Well I certainly don't have time for this bullshit."

"Okay...then we'll let you be next in line."

Chopper thumbed the button on the six-coloured ballpoint and walked toward Murphy's truck. "Are you carrying any liquor at all?"

Norris

It was an early morning in May when the red pickup truck pulled into the muddy yard and stopped beside the house. A young man in a denim jacket and sunglasses got out of the truck. He crossed the yard, mounted the crooked wooden planks that served as front steps to the house and rapped his knuckles on the door. He waited. Out in the junkyard a meadowlark trilled. He knocked again and the door opened. An old woman looked out at him, her eyes crinkled against the sun.

"Good morning, ma'am," he said. "Your neighbour tells

me you might have some pigs for sale."

The woman shook her head. "No...I'm sorry."

"Isn't this Letendre's?"

"Yes, but we don't have any pigs for sale. They're too young." She looked into the house and spoke to someone. "Go clean that up," she murmured. It was gloomy in the house, with the plastic sheeting still covering the windows, and there was the raucous sound of a television cartoon show being played too loud in the background.

A gruff male voice spoke over the TV show. "Who is it Mum?"

The old woman glanced into the house again. "It's nobody!" she hissed. "Go and clean up your room!"

"Should I come back in a week or so?" the young man persisted.

A man about 40 years of age appeared in the door. "What do you want?" He had red eyes and he needed a shave. His hair was greasy black and it stood up in sharp hackles like the feathers on the ravens at the dump.

"I'm looking to buy a little pig," the young man said.

The man looked at his mother. "And what did you tell him, that they're too young?"

She turned and disappeared into the house.

The man opened the screen door and came outside. "They could be the size of Volkswagens and she'll tell you they aren't weaned yet. Goddamned pigs get treated better than I do. How much are you willing to pay for one."

The young man touched his sunglasses. "That depends on how much you're asking."

"Thirty-five dollars," the man said, angrily clearing his throat.

The young man smiled and shook his head. "That's too much."

"What did you say your name was?"

"Sam Morrison, from Keewuttunnee."

The man spat on the ground. "Don't know the name."

"I'll give you $25," Sam said, withdrawing the money from his wallet, holding it out in his fingers. "Cash money."

The man took the money and stuffed it in his pocket. "All right." He closed the screen-door and vaulted like a teenager off the steps.

Sam followed him across the mud yard. They went in the door of a half-fallen barn. It was so gloomy inside that Sam stopped, unwilling to take another step. After a moment or two his eyes adjusted. There were knots and slats missing from the walls and the sunlight leaked in, throwing a stippled pattern on the barn's dark insides. The man was leaning against the door of a box stall, looking down at the piglets. Sam joined him. "Which one do you want?" the man said.

Six small pigs, no larger than fourlegged watermelons, were nosing around in the straw floor of the stall. The mother was passed out on the floor, huge as a beached whale. The smell rising from the stall was sickening. I should get my head examined, Sam thought.

"It doesn't matter, any one of them."

"A big one or a small one?"

"A medium one, I guess."

The man opened the door of the stall and slipped inside. The piglets started to run around the stall and the sow bucked to her feet. Once inside he pushed open another door that led outside and the sow made one quick circle of the stall and then bolted out into daylight, followed by six grunting youngsters. The man reached down and grabbed a piglet as it whirred by and scooped it into his arms. The piglet immediately began to scream, in such a bloodcurdling manner that anyone listening would have thought it was being tortured with hot irons. The man carried it outside and laid it on the tail-gate of Sam's pickup truck and Sam brought some twine and the man tethered its feet. The woman was watching from the door of the house. It looked like she was holding her hand over her mouth but Sam didn't look twice. They spread some straw in the bed of the truck and laid the pig down beside the spare tire. It was no longer screeching but was choking and sobbing and rolling its eyes in horror. Its back legs were covered with excrement.

Sam got in the truck. "Thanks," he said. "I better get it home."

He drove slowly on the way home. It was a gravel road and he checked repeatedly over his shoulder to make sure the pig was all right. After five miles or so he heard it retching and he stopped the truck. It had gotten sick and there was yellow bile on the straw and its eyes were still clenched tight. Sam got a cloth and went down into the ditch and soaked it in the frogwater, then wiped off the piglet's face. "Try not to be such a pig," he said quietly.

Several miles farther up the road he slowed down for a construction crew that was working on a culvert. He pulled to a stop on the shoulder of the road and waved to a large fat man in a hard hat who was wallowing around in the mud of the ditch. "Hey Norris... Come here. There's a lady here in the back of the truck that wants to meet you."

The man gave Sam a skeptical look. He grunted and jiggled as he climbed up the embankment and looked into the back of the truck. "Holy Jeez," he said reverently. "It's a goddamn pig. Hey look you guys. Sam's got himself a goddamn pig."

The flagman came over. "Hey, nice...what is it, a girl or a boy?"

"You know I never checked," said Sam, dismounting from the truck.

The flagman looked. "It's a boy. It looks a lot like Norris. Kinda smells like him too."

"That's what I think I'll call him, Norris the Second."

The tubby man laughed, flattered.

Sam took the wet rag and wiped off the piglet's face. It opened one eye and heaved a great self-pitying sigh.

"What are you going to do with him?" Norris asked.

Sam was patting the pig gently on the flank. "Throw a party and eat him," he replied.

Sam owned an island about nine miles north of town. On the map it was designated S-981, and until Sam shelled out fifteen-five in October of last year it was owned by a widow in San Diego, California. The island was located in a wild and uninhabited section of the river. Sam was planning to build a house and live there year-round. He'd wanted waterfront property a bit closer to town but he'd given up on that. All the serviced lots were sky-high and the crown was sitting on everything else. When the island came up he realized he'd be living the life of a hermit but hell, he could go on looking forever too.

There were no buildings on the island and Sam intended to build a log house the following winter. For now he lived in a half-shot old houseboat that he anchored in a U-shaped notch at the south end of the island. The houseboat was temporary lodging, and was getting near the end of its days. It had once belonged to a wealthy car salesman from Winnipeg who had used it as a floating bordello throughout the summer and then in the seventies it was purchased by the people at The Keewuttunnee Marina, who rented it out on weekends to morons who drove it into every reef on the river system, and then Sam bought it for $800, again on the spur of the moment, when the proprietor told him he could pay any time and to please get it away from his dock or he was going to dump a gerry can of gas on it and go looking for a match. The superstructure was made of scaly blue-painted plywood that was slowly delaminating and the glass louvres in half the windows were missing or broken. The floor heaved, the pontoons leaked, the outer deck was rotten and the only method for heating the place was closing the door.

However, Sam filled the living-room with plants, carpets, driftwood artifacts, sea-shells, Bob Dylan posters, bookshelves, animal skulls, stereo-speakers and barnwood furniture and decided it would have to suffice until he got his house built. As soon as the ice went out in the spring he pushed it out to the island with his twenty-horse and nudged it into that U-shaped bay. Then scrambled up into the woods and tied it down to the big pines with half-inch steel cable. Then threw down the gang plank. Then down went the old snow tires into the water, to cushion what remained of his flotation. The houseboat floated on a pair of steel pontoons, 32 feet long. The pontoons were painted with black tar and horribly rusted. Each pontoon was divided into eight compartments, and so many of the compartments were punctured and waterlogged that all he had to do was stroll down one side of the houseboat, clinging to the narrow walkway, and the old tub would heel over and almost dump him into the snags and lily pads, where dwelt leeches and dock spiders the size of his hand. Home sweet home.

Sam wasn't weighed down with a great need for human company but he liked the odd visit and conversation as much as the next guy. After spending a few weeks hard at work clearing the site, burning brush, dropping trees, he decided he'd invite all the townies out for a little party. He was browsing through a northern cookbook that night and he spotted a recipe for roast pig. A momentary image came to him, of a stuffed porker turning on a spit above a bonfire, with music, drinks, a big summer moon, barefoot girls and so on and so on...there was no need to search further for a concept.

When he got home that day with Norris the piglet he cleared out a space in the tool-room of the houseboat, laid down a bed of newspapers and put the piggy inside with a bowl of grain and a bucket of water. "Make yourself at home," he said. He closed the door of the tool-room and went outside and got his tools together to build a pigpen. The island was sixteen acres, about the size of a large city block. From the water's edge it rose in a series of granite ledges to a long humpback of open meadows and heavy mixed forest. Sam went to a shady opening in the side of the forest and began building the pen. Using two-by-sixes, ardox nails and a quartet of standing spruce trees he built a square corral with the approximate dimensions of a very small room. With two sheets of plywood he fashioned a low roof. By mid-afternoon he was standing there admiring his work. Not bad. He'd lived in worse places himself. He went down to the houseboat to get Norris, who seemed to be adjusting nicely, curled up and sleeping in a corner of the tool-room. He hadn't even dirtied the floor. Sam carried him up to the pen and Norris snuffled around in the straw. Welcome to your new home boy. You won't be needing a door.

The word soon got out that Sam was raising a pig on the island and people began coming out to visit. At first the boats would troll slowly up to the houseboat, the people standing and waving tentatively at Sam as courtesy demanded, but as these people brought other people and the other people brought friends of their own some of the courteous behaviour began wearing away. Sam would step out the front door of his houseboat and he would hear voices up in the woods—more visitors. The police boat came by one day and bubbled hesitantly a hundred yards off shore until Sam waved them in. Chaput and Murphy tied the big inboard up to the tail of the houseboat and came aboard. The two big guys coming up the narrow walkway heeled the houseboat over and Sam had to yell a warning and they almost got dumped into the water. They leaped from the houseboat onto the shore and Sam led them up into the woods. Norris, the local hero, peered up at them from the churned earth upon which he lay. His ears hung over his eyes like a coy hairdo. Murphy was of course an authority on swine management and he told Sam how to custom-feed Norris for that extra poundage. They all stood there silently for several minutes, watching. The smell of the black earth

138

and the small fly-bothered pig was not unpleasant. Sam cleared the air by mentioning that they were both of course invited to the barbecue. "Hey, all right," said Chaput. Murphy asked who was going to dispatch Norris when slaughtering day came.

"I will," said Sam.

Murphy offered his services. He said he'd done it many times before.

"Okay. If I change my mind I'll let you know."

"This is the spot," said Murphy. He drew his service revolver and flipped Norris' earflap out of the way and stuck the gun muzzle right into the ear. "Bang," he said. "Out go the lights."

Sam went into town for a bag of nails one day and when he came back he saw a dirty old freighter canoe with an ancient Johnson six-horse pulled up on the shore on the north side of the island, half concealed by the shadows and undergrowth. He knew who owned the boat and he didn't waste any time motoring around to the other side. Smelly Mike and Johnny No Cash were standing beside the pigpen when he got there. Smelly Mike was wearing a big hunting-knife on his belt and they both looked a bit guilty. "Thinking of having a pork chop for lunch?" Sam asked, with a big smile. They both laughed, as if this were the funniest thing they had ever heard. Sam went about the business of watering Norris and changing his straw and when it became apparent that he wasn't in the mood for inviting them to the barbecue they made their excuses and headed for their canoe. Sam didn't trust either of them. Johnny No Cash was a ratfaced and ponytailed little item who'd wandered in off the highway one day with his guitar in a black plastic garbage bag. Like a lot of people in Keewuttunnee he came from somewhere else, somewhere else where he had a proper Christian name and a social insurance number and so on, but here in Keewuttunnee he only had his guitar, which he strummed in a futile bid for spare change so everyone called him

Johnny No Cash. Smelly Mike was a big man with broken knuckles and a soft voice. He was a biker from Oshawa who'd been here for two years, claiming that he'd be gone just as soon as he got the bread together to get his motorcycle fixed. He had a weedy blond beard and fat arms and wore those paratrooper pants with pockets and zippers all over them. The little Indian kids in town had been responsible for naming him. Whenever Mike walked by they held their noses and whispered to each other. "That guy's kinda *smelly, or something'.*" Sam got into the habit, afterward, of locking Norris into the tool-room whenever he went to town for the afternoon.

Sam had had sloppier roommates than Norris. Without any prompting whatsoever the piglet always desisted from fouling the floor of the tool-room. When Sam got home and unpacked the groceries Norris would explore the forbidden territory of the living-room, or scratch at the door and grunt if he had to go out. He would sit obediently while Sam ate his supper, and if Sam offered him a morsel he would first sniff at it with his pink nose and then take it into his mouth as delicately as a cat. There was always a great display of pleading and whining when Sam closed him into his pen for the night and Sam was beginning to wonder how much pork he was going to be eating on the night of the barbecue. He decided to include lots of cobbed corn and baked potatoes on the menu.

At first he'd planned to invite people on an individual basis, to keep the thing from turning into a natural disaster, but a roast pig party wasn't easy to keep quiet. It seemed that everyone he met either wanted an invitation or already assumed they were coming. Lemon the bartender was working on posters and Sam couldn't bring himself to disapprove. Lemon had taken some art courses at the university and he was Keewuttunnee's resident *artiste*. He was developing a limited series of prints that would forever commemorate the event. One of the posters depicted a baccha nalian feast, with Norris impaled dripping on the spit and dozens of half-clad revellers dancing around the fire. Another poster showed a handcuffed Norris being smooched by officer John Murphy, whose nose looked slightly more rounded and porcine than usual. Burt Harrison had likewise appointed himself music chairman, and he was planning to come out any day with his thousand-megaton stereo system and wire the island for sound. Sam dreaded the prospect of Burt rupturing their eardrums with his Iron Maiden and Ozzy Osbourne tapes but no-one else was probably willing to transport their precious stereo equipment out to the island to be nailed to trees and walked on.

Meanwhile Norris was enjoying increasing freedom. He was spending a lot of time running free every day and Sam thought it would be good for him. He could get away from the biting flies and supplement his diet with the roots and truffles that grew wild in the woods. Visitors always commented on his increased size and Sam himself noticed, especially when he was lifting the pig in and out of the pen. He wasn't getting much fatter but he was certainly taller, with an adolescent's long legs and all the standard identity problems. One day a group of dogs arrived with a boatload of visitors and Norris reacted as if these were his long lost brothers and sisters. The dogs tore back and forth on the island, barking at squirrels, investigating rabbit holes, splashing in the lake, and Norris did his best to keep up with them. He could run almost as fast as they could through the woods but the moss-covered rocks at the water's edge defeated him. The dogs would wade in up to their chests, slap the water with their pink tongues, and then shake off and dash back into the woods. Norris would still be skidding and scrambling at the water's edge, falling on the greasy rock and squealing pitifully. For days afterward, when Sam patted him on the flank he would wag his tail.

Sam was having a lot of trouble figuring out how to make

a rotisserie. His first option was to dig a barbecue pit, Hawaiian style, and bury the body in hot coals overnight. Checking around the island though, he couldn't find any suitable place with deep enough soil to dig a pit. He talked to the alcoholic cook at the hotel and learned that an above-ground barbecue pit, with Norris turning regularly over the coals for twelve or fourteen hours, would probably do the job. This still left the job of designing a spit to turn him on. A dry wooden pole would probably burn from the heat of the fire. A green wooden pole would probably sag under Norris' weight, which was getting close to a hundred pounds by now. Any kind of pole would have to be equipped with clamps of some kind, so the carcase wouldn't slip as the pole turned.

Sam finally swallowed his pride and went to see Smelly Mike, and asked him if he would weld up a set of clamps and a spit. Smelly Mike, knowing that this meant he would be invited to the party, was more than pleased to assume this important role. He and Sam went to the dump—he really did smell bad that day—and cannibalized an old Datsun, knocking off the drive shaft and radius rods and wheel rims and tossing them in Sam's pickup. Back in Keewuttunnee, at Steve's Esso, Murphy and Henry Yelle and Steve the Grouch and Sam stood around watching as Smelly Mike put on his gear and fired-up and arc welded all that butchered steel into a reasonable approximation of a rotisserie stand, with the uprights standing in the wheel rims and the drive shaft as a cross bar. Smelly Mike triumphantly removed his hood and the others stood there muttering in admiration as the steel cooled. Murphy, in uniform, planted his ass on the crossbar and gave it his full weight. Steve the Grouch said that if that didn't break the rig nothing would.

All that week volunteer workers showed up at the island, using his tools, stringing lights up in the trees, cutting down logs for bench seating around the fire and even cutting a small room-sized area out of the forest that featured a

Christmas-light entranceway and a tin foil sign that said DANCE HALL. Burt Harrison came out and started wiring up all the trees with sound equipment: hi-fi speakers, car-door speakers, tweeters, woofers, Eatonia shelf speakers salvaged from the dump, even a set of PA horns from the community hall. He set up a little orange tent in the bush and built the stereo inside, the chrome multi-dialed amplifiers and boosters and spilled guts of cord. Sam patrolled the job site, trying to ensure that any damage done to the local ecology was not permanent. Norris went around making friends with all his executioners. It was almost dark when they finally left.

The next day Sam went up to the terrace in the middle of the island and worked on the site plan for his house. The preparations for the pig roast were almost complete. Norris grazed in the undergrowth while Sam drilled holes in the rock for his foundation footings. The site was 40 feet above the water and he could imagine he was standing on his sundeck, gazing across the miles. Back in the bush there he'd put his pumphouse and wood shed, and maybe a little barn for his animals. On the slope here, there'd be a winding staircase down to the water and the dock, the boat.

When he finished drilling the footings it was seven in the evening. He went for a swim and fed Norris, then made himself a salami sandwich and went and sat on the shoreline with his sandwich and a Coke. Norris joined him. The execution was scheduled for tomorrow morning at eight and the sky was suitably ominous. Norris didn't seem concerned. Sam, with his blue-jeaned legs stretched out on the moss-crusted granite finished his meagre supper and scratched Norris between the ears. Norris snuffled and wriggled his nostrils. They watched dusk come to the lake. The water was slack and one shade lighter than the storm-bruised sky. A loon was whooping maniacally somewhere down the lake. If it rains, Sam thought to himself, we might have to cancel the party. And if we cancel the party, I doubt if we'll go to

143

all the trouble of scheduling it for another weekend. That's the only chance for a reprieve I think you've got, boy.... Until then I think we'll just keep you in your pen.

Next morning dawned bright and clear. Sam didn't waste any time lying in bed. He went up to the woods and found the wall of the pen smashed down and Norris gone. Accustomed to having his freedom, Norris had obviously taken exception to being penned up like an animal. Sam fashioned a lasso at the end of a 30-foot length of yellow polypropylene and looped it, Roy Rogers style, over one arm. He filled a pail with grain and tiptoed into the woods. "Norris? Norrrr-is."

He spotted the pig almost immediately. Obviously unaware that this was a life-and-death matter Norris didn't even flick an ear as Sam slipped the noose over his head. As soon as the rope tightened on his neck though, some ancient and infallible swine-alarm circuit blew in his brain and he suddenly stiffened, loosed a wild squeal and bolted, hitting the end of the slack rope at full speed and burning a fast angry furrow in Sam's palm. Sam swore and dropped the rope and the pig galloped into the woods, with 30 feet of yellow rope bouncing after him. When the execution squad arrived half an hour later—Murphy and Lemon and in one boat and Johnny No Cash and Smelly Mike in another—Sam was kneeling at the water's edge, bathing his wounded hands in the water.

Lemon grounded the bow of his Starcraft and Murphy leaped out. Murphy was wearing a sweatshirt with torn-off sleeves and sunglasses. The handle of a revolver protruded from the waistband of his jeans. "Did you grease him yet?"

"Not yet."

"Do you want me to do it?"

"We'll have to catch him first."

Sam led them up to the pen and showed them how Norris had broken the two-by-six planks as if they were made of balsa wood. "You can't leave spaces or they'll bust out every time," Murphy said. They organized into one-man scouting teams. Sam drew them a map of the island in the dirt.

"He likes to stay in the woods during the heat of the day," Sam explained. "He's got a long rope on him already. Once you spot him, call out for reinforcements."

"I got my reinforcements right here," said Murphy, patting the revolver.

"Yeah great, but don't start shooting holes in the spare ribs."

Sam directed Johnny No Cash and Smelly Mike to the swampy end of the island. Murphy was to come in on a pincer movement from the north end. "He knows me, so I'll take the middle," Sam concluded. Lemon was already off in the bush somewhere, scouting.

Sam gave everybody ten minutes to get into position. He began working his way stealthily into the woods. Soon he was in the gloom of the early morning forest and there wasn't a sign of life. The ankle-deep moss sank underfoot and the ferns hung down. This is my island, he thought to himself. I own it. I own all these trees. I own Norris the pig. A frond of underbrush waved back and forth and he spotted Norris' curly-trailed rump sneaking away. The rope was no longer around his neck. He frowned. He called out, "It's an island, Norris."

They combed the island for two hours and only spotted Norris twice. The first time when Sam spotted him. The second time Murphy got a shot. Murphy was of course a marksman of almost frightening skill but on this occasion he muffed a running shot at twelve paces. "Pretty small target," remarked Sam. Murphy and Smelly Mike and Johnny No Cash and Lemon went into town to have breakfast, swearing that they would return with reinforcements in several hours.

"Don't worry Sam," Smelly Mike said, giving Sam a consoling pat on the shoulder, as if a tragedy had come to his family. "We'll hunt him down."

145

Apparently after breakfast (more like lunch) they got temporarily sidetracked into the bar and spent several hours slaving over a hot pool table. It was late in the afternoon when they returned, with a flotilla of drunken reinforcements, and Sam had already started the fire up on the hill. Smelly Mike was wearing cutoffs and a Harley Davidson shirt and was carrying a peeled spruce pole with a hunting-knife lashed to the end of it. The others were carrying a motley assortment of weapons. Burt Harrison, stylish as usual, looked like a besotted Mexican road agent. His hair was swept back in a wild mane and he wore his shirt like a cape and he was grinning and brandishing a gaff hook. "I wouldn't go to a lot of trouble," said Sam. "It's too late to cook him now anyway."

"Hey man," Burt Harrison crooned. "It's never too late."

"It takes twelve hours, minimum, to roast a pig and it's almost six o'clock now."

Smelly Mike checked the lashing on his spear. "Yeah, but this is a question of honour."

"Right on," somebody replied.

Smelly Mike nodded. "A question of honour...RIGHT BOYS?"

There was a cheer and a waving of knives.

"Suit yourself," Sam replied. "But I'm going to start cooking the corn and potatoes."

"Oh man, look at these beers on ice."

"We'll have ONE drink," Smelly Mike decreed.

"He usually comes back for his grain at mid-day," Sam shrugged, explaining the pig's absence to Sonny. "I haven't seen him since first thing this morning."

Burt Harrison had stumbled his way into the stereo tent. There was a horribly amplified scratch and sizzle from the trees and then the first chord struck, loud as a crashed helicopter.

"ONE DRINK," Smelly Mike reiterated. Nobody was listening to him.

More boats were arriving. These ones, thank God, containing a moderating element of females. Sam tipped his head slightly to avoid the swung knife-tip of Smelly Mike's spear. He glanced at Sonny. "So tell me…you read any good books lately?"

All night long there were torchlit forays into the bush to look for Norris. Dim Harrison fell on his machete and the last thing Sam knew was that they took him back to town, bleeding profusely from the web of the hand. Johnny No Cash fell in the bonfire, for the second time this summer, and he didn't seem to be burnt too bad though it wasn't easy for Leslie the Indian Affairs nurse to give a physical examination to a smoking, semi-conscious drunk by flashlight. By two in the morning the beer supply was exhausted and a lot of people were heading for home. The nicer people came by and thanked Sam for the party and a lot of them admitted they were a bit leery of the pig-roast idea anyway. The corn and the potatoes were a better idea. Vegetables don't have first names. Smelly Mike and a few others loitered around the fire until very late but Sam gave up and went to bed. Finally, in the chill part of the morning, when the first squirrels were ratcheting in the forest and the bass were splashing around the houseboat Sam heard Smelly Mike coming through the woods and climbing the gang plank of the houseboat. Everybody had left without him, Smelly Mike had fallen asleep and now he was mumbling, shivering and stumbling his way toward his freighter canoe, which he'd left tethered to the back of Sam's houseboat. Sam felt the houseboat tilt gently as Smelly Mike made his way down the side. He heard the muffled exclamation of alarm as the houseboat kept tipping, and heard the helpless clawing of fingernails on plywood and the long instant of silence and then the sudden, booming killer-whale splash. Sam smiled, how nice. He lay in bed, faking sleep, while Mike clambered out of the water sputtering and screaming profanities.

147

When the drone of Smelly Mike's freighter canoe faded around the corner Sam got out of bed and tiptoed outside. Up on the hill he could see the littered beer cans and paper plates and ungreased Datsun spit. That's my party, he thought. That's the last party I'll be having for a while. He opened the door of the tool-room and let Norris outside. The pig scooted down the gang plank and urinated, with a great groan of relief, against a bush.

Sam shivered in the sharp morning air. "Go and clean up that mess," he said to the pig. "And don't say I never did anything for you."

Reuben

Like a beefsteak beaten with a mallet, like fruit pulp frozen and thawed, the weary little northern Ontario town seemed damaged right down into its fibre. With a dizzying flash of heat the month of May caught the village still half-dressed in its dirty winter clothes. Dead grass, rusted cables, wadded bird carcases, cookie wrappers, dog feces, swollen mucky roads; they all baked like a great snow-bandaged open wound under the brassy glare of the spring sun. It was a Saturday morning when the waxed and shiny OPP cruiser pulled into the fouled mud lot of the Hudson's Bay store.

Inside the police car Constable Alain Chaput, age 25, and Constable John Murphy, age 43, sat in the idling car and watched the patrons entering and exiting the store. Some of the patrons were old Indian women, in scarves and billowing skirts, but most of the store's customers were school-aged Indian youngsters, who stood in the doorways with their bags of Cheezies and cans of orange Fanta and ganged and fussed with each other and ignored the police car, which was a normal component of their landscape in any case.

Behind the wheel John Murphy scratched his blond, furry bull's head. One of his hands was draped disdainfully over the rim of the steering-wheel. The other knuckled fist propped up his fleshy, sleepy-eyed, fed-up policeman's face. Across the seat from him his partner, Alain Chaput, was tearing open two envelopes of sugar and stirring them into his coffee. He was using the open door of the glove compartment as a little table. Murphy shut the car off and in the abrupt silence there was only the sigh of the turd-scented spring wind, and the sporadic mutter and snap of the police radio.

Murphy glanced at his watch, and irritably tapped it with his finger. "What's the friggin time, anyway," he asked. John Murphy seldom used question marks.

Chaput looked at his own watch. They were supposed to rendezvous here with a third policeman, an Indian probationary constable they were training, but he was late. "As usual," Murphy grunted.

"It's 10.16," Chaput said.

Murphy grimaced and lit a cigarette. "Chopper, that dingbat. I'm gonna really give it to him this time...."

Constable Chaput nodded, only half listening. He was looking at a youngster who was sitting on the muddy ground at the side of the store. The youngster had his back against the concrete foundation of the store, and he was casually returning Chaput's stare. Chaput recognized him as the same one he'd picked up hitch-hiking the other day.

He'd been off-duty at the time though, and the kid probably didn't remember him.

Chaput stared at the kid for another couple of minutes, and the kid stared back. He glanced at Murphy, who was reading a couple from his cigarette pack. Murphy's lips were moving, and there was a crumple of cigarette ash on the lap of his uniform. Chaput looked back at the youngster, and once again they exchanged a mutual long gaze. Chaput smiled, but across 50 feet of muddy parking-lot the smile had no effect. Finally Chaput lifted his hand, and mimicking a pistol he thumbed a shot in the youngster's direction.

The reaction was immediate. The little boy, who looked only ten or eleven years old, got to his feet and walked toward the police car. He was a Metis boy, half-white, half-Indian. His clothing was ragged, almost clownish. His dirt-stiffened trousers were slashed at the knee, his shirt was missing most of one sleeve. With his flat, pugnosed face, weedy chestnut hair and comically sturdy gait he looked like a little prize-fighter. He was carrying a family-sized Fanta in his fist.

Finally he stopped about three feet away from Chaput's open window. In one of his grubby little hands he held a burning cigarette, not much more than just a smouldering filter. In the other hand he held the neck of the Fanta bottle. Stopping, staring at Chaput with narrow, inscrutable eyes he took a pull on the burning cigarette, then slowly lifted the huge bottle straight up and began to drink, gulping noisily, dreamily, interminably, until all of the neon-coloured liquid drained down into his bobbing throat. Then he broke the bottle away, empty, and issued a loud satisfied belch. Louder than necessary.

He stared at Chaput. "You try to shoot me, eh?"

Chaput smiled. "Don't you remember me?"

Reuben shook his head. "I don't talk to no dirty cops."

Chaput glanced at Murphy. Murphy leaned across the seat. "Reuben…would you come here for a moment?"

"I can shoot too," Reuben continued, glowering at Chaput.

Chaput smiled uncomfortably. "I'm sure you can."

Murphy was easing open his door. "Reuben, come here. I want to talk to you."

Reuben retreated, walking slowly backward. He pointed at Chaput. "Next time don't try to shoot me or maybe I'll shoot you."

After that meeting Chaput began to see him everywhere. His name was Reuben, and he was one of the toughest and most energetic youngsters in Keewuttunnee. He was often alone, out of choice. He would stand apart, brooding like a general. When the school buzzer rang at noon Reuben would always be the first to burst out the double doors, warbling an Ojibway war cry and sprinting like a little machine for the hockey field. He was a muscular 60 pounds and seemed absolutely fearless. If there was an immense uproar during a game of field hockey it was usually because Reuben had just made a breakaway or scored a goal or started a fight (playing against fifteen-year-old boys twice his size, they would complain to the teachers that Reuben was playing too rough). And when the buzzer went at one o'clock Reuben was usually the last one to obey it, sometimes loping up and down the hockey field all alone, vigorously slapshooting stones into the long grass, swivelling his hips to evade imaginary enemies and blithely ignoring his teacher's shouted summons until the pitch of her voice rose to a near-shriek, at which point he would slap one last stone down the field and trot casually toward the door. One day, several weeks after their first meeting in the store parking-lot, Chaput was parking in front of the school, watching the kids, when Reuben was pulled out of the game for roughing. The schoolteacher, an obese young woman in pigtails, strode up to Reuben and grabbed his arm, and Reuben spun around and punched her in the stomach.

Chaput, behind mirrored sunglasses, watched from afar.

Furious, rubbing her wounded stomach, she shouted that he was to go inside. Reuben walked ten feet, then turned and gave her the finger. And then as he walked toward the door of the school he spotted Chaput sitting in the cruiser. Slightly altering course he walked over to the car and kicked it vehemently in the tire, then strolled up to Chaput's window.

"Hurt your foot?" Chaput inquired.

Reuben stood with his hands on his hips, staring fiercely into Chaput's neutral face, his mirrored eyes. "You're a dirty cop, you know."

"Am I?"

Reuben nodded. "Got a smoke?"

"I might give you one, but you're pretty young to smoke."

Reuben shrugged. "Screw you then." He reached into his shirt pocket and extracted a withered cigarette butt and a match. He lit the wooden match on his zipper and cupped the cigarette so that the teacher wouldn't see it. He studied Chaput. "I'm not s'pose to smoke here you know."

Chaput lit a cigarette on the car lighter. "I know."

"My brother's not afraida cops you know."

"Who's your brother?"

"He's got a nice .22. He taught me how to shoot it. I could shoot cops easy."

Chaput blew smoke wearily, looked at Reuben, almost as tall as the door-handle. "Don't say things like that."

"Reuben!" yelled the schoolteacher. "ARE YOU SMOK-ING!?"

Reuben threw the cigarette butt at the onrushing school-teacher and ran across the field, swivelling his hips, feinting and dogging like a jackrabbit, with the fat woman shrieking and clawing air two strides behind him.

Several weeks later school let out. The teachers vanished to their homes in the south. The kids slept all day, swam in the river, the schoolyard echoed with their whooping every night until dawn. Sergeant McCandless and his wife went on summer holidays. Constable Voth broke his collarbone water-skiing behind the police boat and was sent back down south. The Indian constable was supposed to replace him anyway. Murphy and Chaput were left to patrol the township. One day Chaput was sitting in the office when Murphy walked in, wearing a golf jacket and jeans.

"Hi Al. Hey listen I heard a good one today. What's black and brown and looks nice on an Indian?"

"I don't know."

"A Doberman Pinscher."

"Really."

"Yes Al, really. What are you typing?"

"Benny Bird's common assault. He beat up his girlfriend."

Murphy peered over his shoulder. "Jezuz, Al, you never tell me nothin'."

Chaput pulled the complaint out of the typewriter and handed it to Murphy. Murphy tossed it on the desk without looking at it. "So where's my coffee?"

"In the jar."

"Yeah sure, I have to do everything around here. Oh— that'll be the phone."

Murphy snatched the phone and sat on the edge of the desk. "Ontario Provincial Police. Constable Murphy speaking. Oh yeah, uh-huh...good, okay... Thanks, we'll get back to ya."

Murphy hung up the phone and lifted a set of car keys off the hook above the bulletin board. "Gotta run, Al. I'm taking 302 for an hour."

"Like hell. You're not even working today. And I need wheels so forget it."

"I'll bring it back in half an hour."

Chaput glowered at him. "Okay, take it. But you have to drop me somewhere first."

"Will it take very long?"

Chaput stood up and put on his hat. "It won't take as long as it would if you were walking."

Murphy lifted a hand. "Okay, okay...where are you going?"

Chaput stalked past him. "East end," he said.

They went out the door. It was a warm Saturday. The sprinkler was chattering on the crew-cut front lawn. The beacon and siren-bedecked patrol car they called 302 was parked on the smooth asphalt driveway, facing the road. From the rear bumper dangled ten pairs of tiny running shoes, tied by their laces. "What the hell is this?" Murphy pointed.

"Never mind."

"Aw come on, Al, tell me. What is it? Did you capture the Dinkie Dalton gang?"

"No, the kids were gas sniffing down by the river this morning, so I picked them up and drove them five miles out of town, and now they're walking back barefoot."

Murphy got in the car. "Hey! I like that. It's fair but cruel. You're starting to show real promise."

"So I have to go check on them. They should be halfway back to town by now."

They drove out past the school, the HBC store and out onto the rough road that led out of the village. Murphy gunned the patrol car and they swept down the road, a stormcloud of dust unfurling behind them. They drove for several minutes, and the forest and the beaver ponds slipped by. Murphy powered the car through a sharp corner and a group of children caught in the car's path scampered off the road.

Murphy slid the car to a half. "Little buggers. I could have stopped easy."

"Just let me out. Just leave me here," Chaput snapped, getting out of the car.

The dust slowly cleared. In the ditch a small boy was

standing in knee-deep stagnant water. "Hey, ya stupid cops! Can't ya drive or something?"

"Yeah!" said another eight-year-old, stomping out of the long grass toward Chaput. "Shaw-put! Ya stupid cop!"

"Never mind that," replied Chaput, putting his hands on his hips and counting noses. "Where's Pokey? And where's Reuben?"

"Do you want a ride back?" Murphy called out the window.

"No I don't! Where's Pokey and where's Reuben...you kids?"

"He wouldn't walk!" said one little girl. Murphy sprayed gravel, leaving.

"Where's our shoes?" exclaimed another, mincing on the sharp stones.

"Your shoes are back in town. Or in fact...they're tied to the bumper of that police car. If you walk another half hour you'll get them. I'll walk with you."

"You got shoes, ya dirty cop."

"I got shoes cause I'm not a bad gas sniffer like you kids. Every time I catch you sniffing gas you're going to be walking home with no shoes. And even if I *hear* that you're sniffing gas, if your teachers smell it on you, you're going to be out here."

"Even in winter?"

"Even if it's a hundred below, no socks, no shoes. Now there's nine of you...where's Reuben?"

"He wouldn't walk!" exclaimed Pokey. "He said he won't walk until somebody comes and gets him."

"He said he's gonna kill you," said another little girl.

"Never mind what Reuben said. He'll be walking home just like the rest of you. Now get in line everybody...and here comes a car, so stay out of the way."

Chaput herded them to the shoulder as a pickup truck approached. "Have you been doing your confession, when a car goes by? The way I told you?"

"Yeah, yeah..." they answered disgustedly.

The truck thundered toward them and they lined up alongside the shoulder, joining hands. They began to chant, "WE ARE THE SNIFFERS. WE SNIFF GAS. WE ARE THE SNIFFERS, WE SNIFF—"

The chant suddenly erupted into a cheer. Crouching in the back of the truck was the tiny hunched form of Reuben. Jumping to his feet, he emptied an imaginary rifle at Chaput, working the lever, pumping shots into Chaput's face. He shook his fist in the air and yelped a fierce war cry, which Chaput could distinctly hear above the cheering as the truck swept by and disappeared in a pall of dust around the corner.

Summer ended, autumn came. Hallowe'en night was cold and windy. Chaput patrolled the reserve alone, driving slowly up and down the roads, his window cracked open and the heater whispering, but though his headlights picked up the occasional kicked-over garbage can or fleeing pack of vandals the night seemed quiet for Hallowe'en. A dance had been planned for the school but had been cancelled because of technical difficulties; someone had plugged the toilet with paper towels and half the school was flooded. So three hundred kids were out somewhere amusing themselves, but Chaput certainly couldn't find them. He checked the dump in the east end, looking for teenagers parked with their girlfriends smoking hash, and checked the gas-sniffer's fort down at the bottom of the ravine in the west end, but his headlights shining on the fort showed it empty, empty and cold as the gleaming coil of river sliding by beyond. Driving back across the reserve he saw a cigarette glowing on the far side of the football field. He turned the cruiser off the road and drove across the frozen ground of the football field. It was Frances, one of the schoolteachers. He stopped the car and rolled down the window. "Good evening Frances."

"Good evening Constable." She knew his first name but

she addressed him formally as a way of kidding him.

"How are you?"

"Fine." She tapped on her cigarette, loosing a spark. "I think winter is coming."

He nodded. "I agree."

They looked at each other for a few moments; she was wearing just the hint of a smile. Chaput wasn't good at this sort of thing; banter, small talk. He sat there for a while. "So, it's Hallowe'en."

She nodded. "Yes it is."

He sat there for a while. "Seen many of the kids around?"

"Not many."

He nodded. He'd been meaning to ask her for a date, but hadn't quite got around to it. He sat there for a few moments but began to get nervous. He clicked the shifter down into D and kept his foot on the brake. "Well..."

She smiled. "It's been nice talking to you."

"Okay, goodnight."

He drove the circuit of the reserve for another two hours, then went back to the police station. The odd frozen bit of rain, almost snow, gusted into his face as he got out of the cruiser and went into the police station. The warmth of the office, the waxed linoleum, the bright fluorescent ceiling; suddenly he realized how tired he was.

"Quiet evening," he said to Murphy, who was sitting with his boots up on the desk reading a magazine.

"Oh yeah?"

"I'm going to bed."

"Goodnight."

Chaput went out to his trailer, kicked his boots across the room, hung his clothes on the doorknob and went to bed. He'd been asleep for some time, he didn't know how long, when he heard a noise in the room, and then light flooded into the room and he kicked his feet, swimming up out of a deep sleep. "What...what...?"

Murphy was standing at the foot of his bed, throwing him

his clothes. "Come on Al. Come on Al. There's a fire."

In stumbling haste Chaput wrestled into his clothes and hurried out to the car. Murphy was waiting, revving the motor. On the eastern sky was the horrid orange glow of fire. Chaput dived into the front seat and Murphy hit the accelerator.

The fire was on the edge of town. As they sped down the hill and around the corner the house was suddenly there, a perfectly intact frame house encased in a rippling gel of flame. The vivid light illuminated trees and cars and a small crowd of people. Through broken windows in the back of the house white flames hosed out and turned to orange, doubled back and slid up the roof. On a side wall a large propane bottle had blown its top; a dragon's breath of hooked flame shot sideways fifteen feet and swerved up to join the fire on the roof. A mane of stringy flame and sparks gushed off the road and spiralled up into the higher darkness. The front windows of the house were dark and empty, blank as the eyes of a burning skull.

Murphy hit the brakes and they both jumped out.

"Anybody in there?" he yelled at a group of bystanders.

Chaput ran across the driveway. He could hear Murphy yelling at people, trying to find out if the house was occupied. He tiptoed up the front steps, the fire mewing and creaking up on the roof, and tried to peer through a window into the eerie black vacancy within. He touched the door and the handle burned his hand. With his coat sleeve he turned the door handle and kneed the door open. A ball of flame like a giant fist slammed the door closed again, rocking him back with its heat.

He heard a shout from Murphy. "Al! Get away from there!"

Noel Jonnie had arrived on the scene and was standing beside Murphy. They were holding a boy between them, and gesturing for Chaput to join them. The crowd was

159

growing now. A ring of firelit faces watched Chaput as he took one last glance in the window and then jogged down the stairs.

"You people get back," he said. "Come on! Let's move away! This place is gonna really start to go."

"Al, this kid was in the house. They were gas sniffing."

Noel Jonnie nodded. "He says they were sniffin'. Him and the other boys."

"Where are the other boys?"

Noel Jonnie knelt down. "Where are the other boys?"

Noel Jonnie looked up. "He says he doesn't know."

"Ask him if the other boys are in the house."

Noel Jonnie asked the questions. "He says the other boys ran away."

"What started the fire?"

"He says it was an accident, Reuben was smoking and there was gas."

John Murphy spat on the ground. "Well at least nobody burned."

"I guess we better go and find Reuben and his cronies," Chaput said. "You want to stay here and keep an eye on things Noel?"

Once again the boy spoke to Noel Jonnie. They were speaking in Ojibway but there was one word Chaput recognized. "This is bad," said Noel Jonnie.

"What'd he say?"

"He says Reuben stole a gun."

They went back to the police station and got McCandless out of bed while Noel Jonnie stayed at the burning house. They told McCandless the story and when they drove away he was visible through the venetian blinds, sitting on the desk in sweatshirt and blue jeans, pipe clamped in his jaws, talking to district headquarters on the radio.

Murphy and Chaput drove slowly down the dark road. "I don't care how old he is," Murphy said. "If he starts waving a gun around we're going to leave him alone. We'll leave him alone for a day or two…you don't push nobody who's got a weapon, even a kid. Even if he's a close personal friend of yours."

"Yeah, yeah…"

The night wasn't even over yet and Murphy was already rubbing it in. Chaput knew he should be angry at Reuben but he wasn't.

They drove to a few of Reuben's secret hangouts—places that Chaput knew better than Murphy. There were only five or six places he could go, it was that simple.

But no Reuben.

The combed the reserve for an hour. They drove over to Keewuttunnee and back several times, running the spotlight through the roadside trees. The orange glow of the fire faded in the sky and the night moved into its deepest and most uninhabited depths. A broken moon cruised over-head. Herds of leaves blew across the road in front of the car's headlights. Finally they decided to call it a night, and look for the kids the following morning. Murphy's voice made Chaput's heart suddenly jump.

"There they are."

The car leaped, Murphy jabbing the gas pedal.

"Where?"

"Look…there's a bunch of them."

Murphy flipped the dashboard switches and the siren started to whoop, they accelerated. Ahead Chaput saw three youngsters on the road; one stayed on the road, running up the shoulder toward the patch of forest where the tree fort was. As they got closer Chaput recognized Reuben, running like a deer. "Get ready to grab him," Murphy said.

Reuben reached down into the long grass in the headlights and came up with a shotgun, swung around and aimed it, little-boy style, at the onrushing car. The gun barked and spat flame. Murphy slammed a hand against the roof and the car swam wildly out of control, yawing side-ways then re-accelerating into a counterspin almost tipping as its wheels dug in and it banged hard backwards into a sandbank and sat there, motionless, with the red light flipping and the siren whooping like a demented ghoul.

"Are you okay? John...are you okay?"

Murphy came out from under the dashboard. "Yeah."

Chaput climbed from the car and ran back down the road. He almost tripped over Reuben, who was lying face down on the road, shaking and choking. His leg was bent backwards at the knee. Chaput turned on his flashlight and dropped it on the ground beside Reuben and ran back to the car. "Get an ambulance."

"What?"

Chaput dived across Murphy and grabbed the radio mike. "Kenora. Fifty eight three oh two. Kenora! We need an ambulance up here right away."

The radio crackled. "Say again three oh two?"

"It's a ten fifty-two code," grunted Murphy, still feeling his body for shotgun holes.

"TEN FIFTY TWO, for Christ's sake! We need an ambulance! Send it up the road and we'll intercept!"

"Ten-four, three oh two."

Chaput grabbed Murphy and wrestled him upright. "Now Murphy I want you to drive just as fast as... Now come on!" Murphy seemed dazed. "Come on!"

Chaput ran back to Reuben and picked him up off the road. He was so light that Chaput had the sickening sensation that part of him was missing. He avoided looking down at the road and ran back to the cruiser. The motor was whirring uselessly then suddenly it caught and roared to life. Chaput climbed into the back seat with Reuben. Reuben was choking, breath snapping in his throat. "He's having trouble breathing," said Chaput.

Murphy was suddenly normal, gunning the car. "Give him mouth-to-mouth."

Chaput knelt on the floor and leaned over the tiny mouth. "Let's go, John, let's move."

162

"We're on our way," said Murphy, and gravel thundered under the rear wheels.

Twenty minutes later they met the ambulance, saw the throb of its red light as it came up the backside of an oncoming hill. "How is he now?" yelled Murphy, slowing the car.

"He's still having trouble breathing."

Murphy pulled over and flashed his lights and the ambulance stopped. The ambulance attendants got out of their van and jogged toward them. They pulled open the door of the police car and Chaput scrambled out.

"What have you got, a kid?"

"A little boy, about eleven years old. We ran over him with the car. I've been giving him mouth-to-mouth, but he's still not breathing too good."

One of the attendants climbed in and looked at Reuben. He took his pulse. He glanced at Chaput. "He's having trouble breathing, all right. He's stone dead."

Chaput looked at the other attendant. "What did he say?"

The other attendant shrugged. "Sorry, guy...there's nothing we can do."

Chaput reached into the car and grabbed the first attendant by the shoulder of his jacket. He started shaking the man. "DO SOMETHING!"

Murphy was squeezing his arms from behind. "Hey, Al, cool it, come on...."

Chaput broke the hold and spun sideways. He walked backwards, three steps, then stepped forward quickly and put his boot into 302's headlight. He stepped forward again and booted the front grill, then kicked in the other headlight. He was sobbing and kicking the car over and over again.

The other three men stood there watching.

At Christmas time one of the schoolteachers broke down and

was sent back to Burlington. Chaput took the house she'd been renting, a little frame bungalow behind the railway station in Keewuttunnee, just a short distance down the road from the reserve. Friday afternoons everyone in the entire northwestern Ontario region migrated into Kenora for banking, grocery shopping and drinking. It wasn't unusual to go down the aisle in Safeway and encounter an informal gathering of five or six people, exchanging handshakes and gossip beside the California grapefruit. Chaput knew a few local people by now, and after loading up the trunk of his car with groceries he'd walk over to the Kenricia and immerse himself in the smoke-filled comfort of the cocktail lounge, the thunder of the jukebox. Sam Morrison or Willy or one of the Harrison boys would whack him on the shoulder and hand him an anaesthetic in the form of a tall, cool bubbling glass of beer. After a while everything would be just fine.

One night in late February he was driving home by himself, just around dusk, and as he topped a hill his heart almost stopped. There on the road ahead was Reuben, wearing that ragged denim jacket, walking with that same comical tough-guy gait as always. He heard the car coming and turned around and raised his thumb and turned into someone else, not Reuben, just another one of the nameless kids from town. His breath shot frosty and his hands were bare and the collar was turned up against the cold. Chaput drove past the kid without slowing and kept the gas pedal down on the floor and didn't even look sideways at the apparition as he went speeding by.

The Bridge

There was always the bridge. As long as anyone could remember the bridge had been there, pre-dating even the beginnings of the town itself. The bridge was built in 1911, when there was nothing on either side of the river but unbroken forest. The first residents were railway navvies who lived in a chaotic tent city along the bank of the river and worked on the structure. The railway executives, admiring the glittering belt of blue river that seemed to stretch on forever, asked their Indian labourers what "Keewuttunnee" meant. The Indians, in the tradition of an old joke that their ancestors played on passing voyageurs, explained that it meant "good luck is coming." Like the voyageurs, the railway men eventually learned that "Keewuttunnee" actually referred to the fact that this channel of the river was a dead end, and strictly translated meant "dead end," or "cul-de-sac," but by then they had already decided that it was a pretty name for the town, and no-one really cared what the word meant anyway.

The railway drew up grand designs for the future town of Keewuttunnee. Here you had a synapse of a major waterway and a railroad line. Surveyors went out and subdivided the bush for miles around; great sprawling maps declared the existence of East and West Keewuttunnee and the adjacent industrial districts and thoroughfares like Pine Ridge Boulevard that funnelled the busy citizens in and out of residential areas like Riverside Heights. In the ensuing years, while investors waited for the town to catch up with the survey map, many a brood of skunks was raised in the thickets of those nonexistent avenues, many a scrawny wolf lifted its leg against those rusted iron survey pins. The car and the highway had been invented, and freight wasn't being hauled by river anymore.

The town as it exists now is a random glittering complex of wooden shacks, bare rock, Atco trailers, machine sheds, prefabricated government bungalows, liquor store, gas staton, CN station and derelict sockeyed log buildings, their broken tin roofs sagging in the sun. At the time the bridge was under construction the town proliferated in a ragged and disorganized way, a ruff of tents and lacy walkways on either side of the iron bridge's monstrous Victorian span. Later, with the registration of deeds to property, the subtle patterns of social hierarchy began to appear. High on the hill on the east side of the river was the rockiest and poorest land. This was inevitably set aside for welfare cases and Indian reservation. Lower down, amongst the junk-strewn yards and tethered huskies, were the shabby-sided wooden homes of the non-status Indians and halfbreeds and working poor. Lower on the hillsides, near the river, are the gaudy aluminum sided bungalows with the shag-carpeted living-rooms and the satellite dishes in the backyard currently inhabited by the schoolteachers and nurses and social workers and police and small businessmen, Keewuttunnee's equivalent of a ruling class. Along the riverbank, where the ancient broken log cabins of the pre-settlement days crouch in the hum of dragonflies and river, is real estate too choice for mere residential purposes. Marina, fishing-lodge, government pier, float-plane base and Keewuttunnee Bay Inn sit right along the waterfront, the most valuable property in town.

The Keewuttunnee Bay Inn features ten sparsely finished hotel-rooms, a dining-room with bear rugs and moose heads, a snack bar finished in knotty pine and a beer parlour. The only item of decoration in the beer parlour with its formica-topped aluminum-legged tables is a large oil painting of the CNR bridge. In spring and summer the hotel is busy with American fishermen, who rent boats and clog the parking-lots with their Winnebagoes. In autumn the tourists leave, the summer people leave, and the river is silent and empty. Leaves rattle in the bare woods, and an outboard motor outside the hotel means Willy coming to shoot a game of pool, or an Indian on his way back up to the reserve. By Christmas the easiest part of winter has passed—there is less charm to the inexorable down-sift of snow, and the yellow beer parlour windows shine out into the endless winter night.

Lemon, the 30-year-old bartender at the Keewuttunnee Bay Inn, sees the winters come and go. He serves drinks to people like Bobby and Melvina, who sit around talking about Toronto and how they are going to do it right next time. He hears them debating keypunch school, pullout couches, the subway. He sees Bobby's new wardrobe—her scarf, tweed jacket, high boots—and sees Melvina hovering in the background, her shadowlike bovine presence almost completely eliminated by Bobby's vixenish good looks. Across the room from Bobby and Melvina he brings a round for Al Chaput, the off-duty cop, who comes in here like clockwork every Saturday night and pours down the Cutty Sark until he's got that dull gleam in his eye, and then he sets them up for the Harrison boys, the regulars, who are in here every night in their blaze-orange MOTO-SKI jackets, boots flopping, talking loud like they own the place, and banging the pool balls so hard that half the time they fly right off the table. Then Smelly Mike and Johnny No Cash, who steal the tips off the table if you're not quick to collect them, and old Joe Hudson, who's boring the pants of Al the cop by telling him for the umpteenth time about the day he threw the grenade in the window of the Normandy farmhouse and killed seventeen men and a dog, and all the other regulars with their habits and idiosyncracies and petulant little feuds, and then there's Willy...the ex-city boy, working for the CN, who with his curls, his sly wink and amiable Irish heart roves around the bar at will, the bridge between everybody, everybody's best friend.

On the morning that Willy was killed, a Sunday morning in early February, Lemon was in the beer parlour cleaning up the mess of the night before. There had been only one brawl, not bad for a Saturday night, but there was still broken glass and dried blood on the floor and he was mopping it up when he heard the faint but distinct throbbing of a helicopter.

He leaned on the mop and listened. In the plexiglass front of the jukebox his gently potbellied, angel-haired reflection stared back at him.

A moment later there was a gloved thumping at the back door. Lemon lit a cigarette and unlocked the door. Swineton, or Swiny as he was called, stood in the brilliant cold, stamping his boots on the squeaking snow. Breath billowed from his contorted red face. "Will you hurry up and let me in, fer Christ sake? It's freezin' out here."

Swineton's moustache was mushy with frost under a snubbed, bulbous nose. "So...did you hear about Willy?"

Lemon felt something slip in him, cold as an icicle. Whenever somebody said, "Did you hear about so-and-so," it meant bad news.

"He got killed. About twenty minutes ago. Over by the maintenance sheds. Got clipped by the train, I think."

Swiny, with grim deliberation, chalked a pool cue. He was seldom the bearer of important news, and he meant to use this opportunity wisely. Lemon moved to the window, shivered as he gazed out at the frost-rimed morning. He studied the bridge, then the far side of the river, as if his reaction might be located there. He buried his hands in his blue-jeans pockets, stared out at the brilliant winter sun. Finally he shrugged and turned to Swiny. "I heard the helicopter."

"Yeah. We were real lucky that it came in. It was flying in spare parts for the railway, so the foreman says. Mind you, he was dead by the time it got here, but anyways..."

"What happened then?"

Swiny broke the balls. "Uh...I figure he got hit by the train."

More steps came to the door, more knocking. It was Sonny Copenace, looking shaken. He'd seen it happen. "That, uh, steel strapping, eh? That they tied the lumber down with? Well, uh, one of them bust loose and was whipping around, hit Willy in the throat as the train went by. He was lyin' on the ground just flippin' there. Just flippin'."

Lemon shook his head. "That's bad."

Sonny Copenace sat down, lit one of Swiny's cigarettes. "Yeah it's really a bummer, boy. One minute he's walking along there, the next minute, dead."

Then the Harrison boys arrived, announced by the tinny snarl of their snow machines, and they came in the door, now unlocked, and stomped the snow off their boots and strode automatically to the snooker table. But Harrison, his mane of blond hair still tangled from sleep, shook a fist emphatically and announced that "There's going to be some serious goddamned drinking going on today."

Then Bobby and Melvina arrived, both with tearful eyes, reeking of morning makeup, and confirmed that Willy was dead. They had just spoken to the cop. And then a moment later Al the cop arrived in person. His cheekbone was bruised from being punched in the face by a logger a few days ago and his hands were shaking from too much booze the night before, but that was normal. There wasn't much else to do on a Saturday night in Keewuttunnee in the wintertime but drink. Willy had been a close friend of his but Al chose to remain a policeman. Death was his department. As he peeled off his gloves the rakish tilt of his hat remained undisturbed. "When somebody is that white," he explained, with a gallic shrug, "you can't do anything. You just lay the tarpaulin over them."

There was a frown, a silence.

Al the cop sat on the edge of a bar stool and eyed the long glittery upside-down row of whiskey bottles.

Sonny Copenace, who had witnessed the accident, sat down heavily in a chair. "Wow, man...I still can't believe it. I really liked that guy."

"How do you think I feel? I was with him last night," Bobby said. Her eyes were smudged, and there was an unfamiliar hoarseness to her voice. Lemon glanced at her unsympathetically. Already she was playing it up, as if she and Willy had been tragic lovers.

"You mean he came over after I left?" inquired Melvina.

"Whaddya mean, Bobby, he was with me!" Swiny interjected.

Burt Harrison was shooting pool with his brother, talking quietly. "You should go see the blood, eh. It looks like a can of paint all over the snow. I almost horked."

"Well I still don't understand what happened..." mumbled Melvina, twiddling her fingers uneasily.

"You know those steel bands that they wrap the lumber with on the freight train?" Al Chaput responded. "Well one of em was loose and whipping around, eh..."

More people were showing up at the door.

"Listen you guys..." announced Lemon, hoisting his hand. "We can't stay here. I'm not even supposed to be open. Let's go back to my place..."

No-one was listening.

"We might as well," Lemon persisted. "C'mon you guys, listen up, eh? Let's go back to my place. I got some food and booze and stuff and we can have a bit of a party. I think Willy would have wanted it that way. What do you think? We might as well, eh? Hey Burt, you wanna put the damned pool balls down like I'm asking you? Okay?"

Lemon lived in an old cottage, winterized, that looked out onto the frozen river. It belonged to his father, as did the skewed, peeling row of light-housekeeping cabins behind it, and in the summer his father came to Keewuttunnee and operated the whole thing as a tourist camp. Lemon, who had once taken twelve credits in Environmental Studies at the University of Manitoba, had lived for the last three years in Keewuttunnee, his hometown. His original plan had been to hole up in the vacant house for a year or so and save enough money to get out of the bush permanently, but one year had turned to three. Instead of banking money he was now in debt even worse than before, and his disgust with his own incompetence was vast.

By mid-afternoon the party at Lemon's house had become a local event. Everyone in town had heard about it, but not everyone came. As if cloven by an invisible flaw the town split into two halves: those who thought it proper to celebrate Willy's death with a party and those who didn't. Or so it seemed to Lemon, who had been off and on the telephone for the last hour trying to invite girls to the party, only to be greeted by the sepulchral tones of mothers who seemed chillingly disinclined to speak loud enough to be heard above the Rolling Stones on Lemon's stereo. Those who had proper homes with rec-rooms and carpeting and colour television sets stayed home with the curtains drawn. Daughters stared silently at Sunday afternoon homework while mothers' weary voices idled like engines in the kitchen. They disapproved of the party in Willy's honour. Those with no real homes, with only CN bunkhouses or shacks or overcrowded Indian Affairs prefabs to live in came to the party; those they partied with were their only family, and when there's trouble in the family, Lemon thought to himself, you always immediately go home.

The afternoon passed quickly with the crowd swelling, then shrinking, then stabilizing around ten or twelve regulars who patronized the bar. The Harrison boys were in the kitchen, clomping around in their Kodiak boots, knocking over glasses and attempting to fry a huge mass of bacon in a cast iron pot. Lemon watched them uneasily, inclined to interfere but hesitant because of prior experience. Either of them, sober, was capable of being violently anti-social, and when liquor was involved along with the death of a close friend anything could happen. As Burt Harrison said, referring to the quieter mourners on the other side of town. "What do they think we're going to do? Just ignore it? Hah! Willy's dead, and I say there's gonna be some DRINKIN'..."

Lemon slipped out of the kitchen, detecting a whiff of war in the air. Bobby and Melvina were sitting by the fireplace, talking about the apartment they had already picked out, describing the type of wallpaper they'd decided on for the kitchen. Swiny, his head teetering like a boulder on the fatty stump of his neck, snuffled through his nose and guffawed. "You'll never cross that gaw-damned bridge till they carry you out in a box!"

Bobby showed him a contemptuous glance. "Go drink

some more floor cleaner, teenage alky."

"Go hump a pig," he said, jerking a sip from his beer.

"I volunteer," muttered Al Chaput, who had finished his shift half an hour ago and now, in his SKI BANFF sweatshirt was drinking triples and making up for lost time.

Sonny Copenace, so drunk that he looked like he was staggering with fever, came up on Lemon from behind and grasped his elbow. He stared heavily into Lemon's eyes, breathing fumes of vodka and beer. "I wanna talk about Willy," he said. "To you. Jus' to you."

"There's nothing to talk about." said Lemon.

"That's right..." declared Burt Harrison loudly. "We ain't here to talk, we're here to DRINK!"

Lemon felt like getting out of the house. He put on his parka and boots, went down the steps and outside, into the winter dusk. The cold air rammed into his lungs and a cough tore out of him as he walked to the woodshed. He reached inside and threw two jack-pine logs on the snow, took the axe off the wall to split them. "Gonna be a cold night, Willy boy," he said aloud.

The frosty steam of his statement hung in the air, proving he'd said it. He swung the axe listlessly and the block split into four. "Thanks," he said aloud.

He leaned on the axe and looked across the yard, across the blue fringes of shadow on the snow, at the smudged hemorrhage of sunset on the distant toothy ridge. Willy, or Will, as Lemon and a few others called him, had probably been his best friend. But then everybody thought that Willy was their best pal. He'd come here by choice; he'd liked it here. He liked the people, he liked the woods and he didn't have the split running through him.

Lemon halved the second block of wood, then straightened his back and looked through the yard. I'll never find it out here, he thought to himself. I never would have believed that my best friend could get killed and I wouldn't even feel sad about it.

173

It was midnight. Bobby's father had come to get her but she had made a furious speech and ended up crying. And Bobby's father had yelled that none of them had any respect for the dead and then he told Burt Harrison he was going to punch him in the face, and Burt only laughed. And then her father left and Bobby went down to the river to play ball hockey. Diana Highway, Sonny's wife, had come to get him but he was too drunk and started crying, so she had stayed, and now they were both down playing ball hockey on the slick black ice of the river. Swiny was in goal, and he was using two cases of beer for goalposts. Sergeant McCandless had come looking for Al the cop, acting very grim and unfriendly because of some mistake that Al had made in the accident report, but Al, who had possibly been sentenced to the Keewuttunnee detachment for having a casual attitude in the first place, hid in the bedroom with Melvina and didn't come out for quite a while after the sergeant was gone. Now Al and Melvina were both down on the ice with the rest of the people playing ball hockey, adding their whooping and applause to the general tumult whenever someone heard an audible crack in the current-teased, treacherously thin ice. Occasionally Burt Harrison or one of his similarly demented cousins would jump up and down on the ice, claiming to test it, but so far no mishap had occurred.

Lemon, winded, clutching a stitch in his pot belly, climbed up the snowpacked riverbank and sat with his back against the foot of the bridge. He coughed into his mitt, and drew a bottle of brandy from his parka pocket. Mist billowed off the mouth of the bottle as he took a sip. Burt Harrison scrambled up the snowbank and sat heavily down beside him.

"Gimme that," he said, taking Lemon's bottle.

He guzzled, gasped. They exchanged cigarettes. Mist, sparks, smoke rolled upwards in the icy air.

"This party goes all night," decreed Burt Harrison. Lemon felt that there was an unspoken agreement among all of them that the party was cancelling out Willy's death. As long as the party endured, then Willy was really here.

"You're a good shit, Lemon."

Burt Harrison seldom spoke to him, but earlier, in a competition to see who could best fall headfirst down the stairs in the house, Lemon had made a number of superbly executed suicidal dives, surprising even himself and winning Burt's favour.

"I'll tell you Lemon...how long have I known you for?"

"Uh...Grade 1 would you believe?"

"What...since that long? Well I don't care what anyone says, you're not a bad guy."

Lemon tapped his cigarette, watching sparks twirl down into the snow.

"An' when I get my dealership in Calgary, I want you to come and see me..." he sipped again, expansively, at Lemon's bottle.

"Sure."

Lemon leaned back on his elbows, scanning the deep starry night. Through the criss-crossed girders of the bridge he could see the Milky Way Spill across the sky, and Cassiopeia, and the Bear. He remembered one night, at a campfire in late autumn, when Willy told him about a certain tribe of Celtic warriors who believed that the Milky Way wasn't just a random belt of stars, it was a bridge—a transparent crystal bridge across the night sky. And the bridge went from earth up to heaven, and when you died you crossed that great black bridge. And all those stars, all those legions of stars, were actually the torches of those travellers as they slowly crossed the bridge.

After they killed the bottle Burt and Lemon went down and rejoined the hockey game, on opposing teams. Right away Burt checked Lemon hard and Lemon fell down on his face, nearly breaking a tooth on the ice. Burt laughed, refusing to apologize, and Lemon shrugged it off, surprised that it didn't hurt. Then later Swiny hit Al the cop in the face with his hockey stick, yelling at him that he was a pig and get out of his crease, and then when Swiny saw the blood he started crying, but Burt punched him in the eye anyway, and Swiny apologized to everybody, tearfully lifting his arms as if he meant the entire town. Melvina took Al up to the house to fix his cut lip and Lemon went back up on the snowbank and sat down while the game continued. At one point Bobby came up and sat beside him, to see if he would try to kiss her, and he did, so she went down and continued with the game and the night wore on. Whenever anyone was tired they would come up and sit on the snow beside Lemon, and the game would continue, and the night would wear on, and the shouts and yelling from the dire hockey game would lift like sacrificial smoke toward the bridge out of town.

PS
8575
.D6
B7
1986

59,051

DATE DUE
